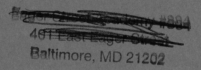

Also by Bruce Brooks

THE MOVES MAKE THE MAN
MIDNIGHT HOUR ENCORES

NO KIDDING

NO KIDDING

BRUCE BROOKS

HARPER & ROW, PUBLISHERS

Grand Rapids, Philadelphia, St. Louis, San Francisco, London,

Singapore, Sydney, Tokyo, Toronto

NEW YORK

1817

Library of Congress Cataloging-in-Publication Data
Brooks, Bruce.
   No kidding / Bruce Brooks.
      p.   cm.
   Summary: In his twenty-first century society, fourteen-year-old
Sam is allowed to decide the fate of his family after his mother is
released from an alcohol rehabilitation center.
   ISBN 0-06-020722-1 : $
   ISBN 0-06-020723-X (lib. bdg.) : $
   [1. Alcoholism—Fiction.   2. Family problems—Fiction.]
I. Title.
PZ7.B7913No   1989   88-22057
[Fic]—dc19   CIP
                                                          AC

Typography by C.S. Barr
2   3   4   5   6   7   8   9   10

For Cokie, and Chickie

Thanks to two true mentors, William A. Caldwell, and Laurence Campbell, both gone now but recalled in every participle and serif.

Thanks also to RK, DJK, DRK, DK, WFK, CCC, KKC, EDC, DTC, AS, RD, DBG, MSW—fellow AO's all.

NO KIDDING

S U N D A Y

O N E

As soon as the boy is gone, the young woman walks over and picks up his coffee cup, holding it down and slightly away from her, and peering carefully inside.

"What are you looking for?" says her husband, sitting across the table.

She looks into the cup for another instant, sighs slightly, and carries it over to the sink. "A clue," she says.

"And what's inside?"

"A coffee stain." She turns the water onto the cup in a stream.

The man chuckles. "You can hardly be surprised. You poured the coffee yourself fifteen minutes ago, and watched him drink every single sip. And I mean *watched.*"

She looks up. Her light-brown eyes are curious. "Did I? Really?"

The man nods. "Yes. You followed every ripple of his throat." He laughs suddenly. It is an easy laugh, quick and honest. "I sound jealous. I *am* jealous, I think. I wish you'd watch *me* that way sometime."

She smiles slightly, then looks down as the water splashes in and out of the cup. "It *is* a different kind of attention, isn't it?"

"You bet," her husband says. "It's . . . it's as if you don't want to blink and miss anything."

"That's it!" she says, looking up. "That's exactly what it is. I watch him—for *everything.* Look: I even examine the things he's touched." She gestures at the cup under the water with a short laugh.

The man nods. "Do you do this so you can understand him?"

She considers. "No. I thought so at first, but I have no hope of that anymore. I think I do it so I can't blame myself for *not* understanding him. Remember when I flunked microtech chemistry my junior year?

Remember how I didn't feel bad about it? That's because I did every single assignment and spent more hours in the lab than anyone. I knew I had given myself every opportunity to pass. That's how this is. That's how I am with Sam."

"I wish it were as simple as microtech." The man laughs. "I got a B in microtech."

"Do you know why he came here today?" She turns to face him.

"Well, I suppose just to check up on Ollie and things. . . ."

She cuts him off. "No. He came—you won't believe this—he came to reassure us about the new research published in the current issue of the *Journal of Secondary Education Methodology.* Of course you're familiar with it."

"Of course I'm not." He frowns. "You *are* kidding?"

"I am," she says, "but Sam wasn't. He never kids. Listen. Sam makes it his business to read these journals—not magazines, now; I'm talking about these incredibly academic little things with a subscription of six hundred, God knows where he finds them, probably in the Library of Congress—so he can keep up with contemporary issues that might have something to do with Ollie. That might have *anything* to do with Ollie."

3

The man is shaking his head. "A fifteen-year-old kid reading educational methodology in the Library of Congress," he says. "Come on."

"Fourteen. Sam is just fourteen—his birthday was pretty recent, I think. Anyway, listen: He came across an article in this journal summarizing the results of recent secular intelligence-capability tests on kids in non-AO programs—private schools, of course—versus those enrolled in AO in private schools."

"You mean public," he says.

"No. Most of the private schools have AO now too, apparently, though it's still elective in most. The tests showed some interesting things."

He smiles. "Interesting to us, or just to Sam?"

She smiles back. "To us too. Even if we haven't quite gotten around to reading our copy of *JSEM* yet."

"I *glanced* at it," he says, "but just refresh my mind on some of the data."

She laughs. "It *is* interesting. Strange, almost. I guess the study was run with the usual methods, with tests given to two groups similar in all other ways, and so on. Scores compared and analyzed, all that stuff. And what these tests showed was that AO kids—in private schools, sometimes the same schools as the other test group—are way ahead in math, intertech, and computational communication. But the non-AO kids are equally far ahead in foreign languages, the art matrix, and unaffiliated history."

"All margin subjects."

"Right. Basically, the AO kids do better in the mainstream of the curriculum. The ones without AO do better in the electives."

"The *weird* electives. What about the allied electives—microelectrical, applied biochem, tech history . . ."

"I believe Sam said the non-AO's did worse in all tech-related subjects. When they took them at all."

The man shakes his head. "I don't know. I find this kind of disturbing."

The woman finally turns off the water. "Well, Sam doesn't. That's why he came by—to assure us we shouldn't be concerned. To tell us that he actually *likes* these results, that he feels even better than ever about Ollie being in a non-AO program. I think"—she pauses, wrinkles her forehead, nods—"I think he really hopes the study applies to Ollie—that Ollie is the typical non-AO student indicated by the test results."

"Great—a tech flunky with a wonderful French accent who can paint. Fabulous. Of course I'm not concerned that my foster son is headed for such a life—not at all!"

She smiles. "Sam knew what he was doing by coming over. It's too bad you weren't here for this part; I think he meant the silent message of his visit for you, and obviously it *does* apply."

He frowns. "What 'silent message'?"

She sighs. "That Ollie is his." Her husband starts to sputter, but she shakes her head. "No, don't; he wasn't lording it over us. In fact, he was making a very practical point in an extremely delicate way. He *is* very delicate about such things, you know that. And very fair."

"And very damn big for his britches. What was this practical point he had to make?"

"That we shouldn't do anything to correct what some people might perceive as an imbalance in the effects of Ollie's education. That as far as he is concerned, these effects are fine."

Her husband barks a mock laugh. " 'Some people,' is it? And what did he think 'some people' might do to correct this minor matter of technical ignorance? Send Oliver to the Japanese School?"

She shrugs. "Hire a couple of tutors or something—maybe *from* the Japanese School. I don't know what he imagined we would want to do. But his implication was that we would certainly know about the research, and be concerned." She smiles softly and glances at the cup in the sink. "I'm rather flattered by that, actually."

The man grunts. "Doesn't it strike you as a teeny bit naive—and a teeny bit condescending—that he would suppose all of this? First of all, that the study was worth anything. Second, that it applied to Oliver's school. Third, that we were aware of it, and fourth, that we were about to make some clumsy response?" He stares at her. Then he adds: "Are you certain he wasn't lording? Or at least showing off?"

She sits across from him and runs a hand through her thick, short hair. She shakes her head. "I'm not certain he wasn't showing off a little, no. After all, he—" But she stops and shakes her head again. After a moment she says, "His main reason was what he said it was: to make certain we made no move with Ollie, in case we either heard of this research or—more likely—saw manifestations of it in our own non-AO student. And I guess he did want to 'reassure' us that he is still responsible for Ollie." She looks at her husband. "He's aware that it seems odd for him to be in charge of a child under the care of two adults. He has to keep letting us know he's there and watching. But at the same time he wants us to feel, you know, like parents—"

"We *are* parents," the man says, putting a hand over one of hers. "Ollie's."

She frowns and looks at the table. The man watches her for a full minute. Then he says, "What is it?"

She looks up at him, and down again. "It's close. We're close now, and I guess I'm getting nervous." She nearly pouts. "*You* don't seem nervous at all. I'd almost think you haven't been keeping up, if we didn't mark the calendar."

"I've been keeping up—the probationary year is over on Friday and I know it," he says gently, rocking her hand back and forth. She still frowns. He says, "I was just waiting it out in my way. You're waiting it out in yours. To tell you the truth, I haven't mentioned it lately because you've been so wound up and silent about it; I thought you might be feeling superstitious."

"Just frantic," she says. "Mr. Mellow and Ms. Nerves." She sighs. "I don't care how each of us waits it out as long as it ends up *our* way." She smiles. "I just flunked a parenthood test: I should have said, 'I don't care how we wait as long as it turns out Ollie's way.' "

"You didn't flunk," he says. "You know our way is Ollie's way. We're great for him. And you're not the only one who knows it."

She studies him. "You mean Sam?"

"I mean Sam."

"I suppose he does like us. God, I hope so. I just can't imagine he'd string us along right to the end if he were going to retain. Or—" She frowns deeply.

"Or what?" he says, alarmed at her expression. "What is there besides retaining or giving Ollie to us?"

"Well," she says, "there *is* a mother. . . . I mean, as the final decision comes, I can't help thinking about it. I bet Sam thinks about it too. I *know* he does—he thinks about everything."

Her husband nods almost eagerly. "Yes, but what you said is important—you are thinking about 'it'— about there being 'a mother.' Not Sam. Sam, you can bet, is thinking about *her.* Not 'it,' not about 'motherhood,' but about this *specific* person, with all of her specific qualities. And who knows better than Sam that she is absolutely *not* the right one to bring Ollie up? Sam and Sam alone put her very clearly out of the running. I'd say he made a very wise decision— and that, having made it, he's moved on to the next decision. That's us."

She nods, obviously still troubled. She repeats: "I suppose he does like us."

"Of course he *likes* us. But that doesn't mean a damn thing, as far as his signing over custody. He's spent the last year doing a lot more than becoming our buddy. That little fox has evaluated absolutely everything about this home, with only one standard in mind—Ollie's welfare. I honestly believe he could hate us personally, but would not hesitate to sign his brother over if he thought we were the best parents for him."

She smiles. "He's amazing. You're kidding, but I think you're actually close to right."

"And we are, you know."

"We are what?"

"The best parents for Ollie."

They stare at each other for a few moments; then she nods and looks down. He says, "Is that enough for you?"

"Of course it is," she says. Then: "But I wish I also had a sense of what's best for Sam."

"I thought so," he says. "Of course."

She goes on, vaguely reaching for his empty cup. "A minute ago, when we were talking about showing off, I almost said 'After all, he's only a kid himself.' But I stopped. I almost said it, but I couldn't. Because he's *not* only a kid. You just can't call him that." She tilts the cup, looks briefly inside, and slides it a couple of inches back toward him.

He watches her. "You're right," he says. "He knows too much."

She starts to nod, then switches to a sharp head shake. "No. About the things that *should* count for him, he knows all too little. He knows *nothing* about being a child."

He thinks for a moment, then nods. "No kidding," he says. He thinks for a moment, and laughs once. "Hey, that's pretty good: *No kidding.* Get it?"

She smiles distractedly and nods, dropping her eyes to the table. After a moment she glances up at him and says, "You know, maybe Sam's the one who needs some tutoring."

He smiles slightly, watching her carefully. "In astrophysics? From a five-year-old Master from the Japanese School?"

She smiles ruefully. "No. In childhood. From a couple of thirty-two-year-old Novices from the American Home."

He meets the smile. Then, gently, he says, "I'd like to, of course."

"Me too."

"I like the kid, and I'd love to have him here with his brother."

"So would I." She stares at him hard.

He stares back. Then he puts both of his hands over both of hers. "He'd never come. Think about this. He'd never come back inside a family." She doesn't change her expression. He goes on. "He's

11

beyond it—he couldn't handle being a kid in a household again." The man sighs. "At least, he *thinks* he couldn't handle it."

She hesitates, then nods. "I know," she says. "*Thinks.*" She removes her hands from his, picks up both of their cups, stands, and walks to the sink. "The sad thing is he never had it, really. He's not beyond it—he's never even approached it." She turns on the water. "He'll never know what he's missing."

"Oh, I don't know," says her husband. He watches her for a moment, then looks down and says, "I think he's trying very hard to *be* just what he's missing." But if his wife hears this above the hiss of the hot water, she makes no sign.

T W O

The second-story room is small but bright; large windows in the side and back walls let in the afternoon light, tinted a coppery brown by the winter leaves of sycamore and beech close to the house.

The floor is made of wood that must once have been simply pale; now it is yellow through thick, clear shellac that still faintly perfumes the air, harsh but refreshing. The walls have been painted a bluish white. There are curtains the same color, pulled back.

The door is painted a deep burgundy, very glossy. It opens.

A man's head juts in alongside the tilted edge of a bed frame. He is wearing a green corduroy cap with the words JAKE'S JUKES stitched across the front in yellow letters. He looks quickly around the room. "No way," he says.

A man with curly hair appears behind him. "Don't think it will all fit?"

"No way."

Another voice—a boy's voice—comes up the stairwell behind them: "It will fit. All of it. It's been measured. Just carry the bed in, please."

The men look at each other, shrug, and bring the large headboard into the room. They rest it against the outside wall and stand back, pulling their cloth gloves on more tightly. The white shade of an iron floor lamp appears through the doorway, and behind it comes the boy.

"There's only one outlet," he says, placing the lamp down. "We'll put the bed over here so the light can reach it."

The men nod and heft the headboard. "A reader, is she?" asks the man with the cap. "Likes to read in the sack?"

The boy frowns and ignores the question. "That's good," he says, as the men shift the headboard.

"Now let's get the rest of the frame. Once the bed's in we can place the chairs and tables."

"What about rugs?" asks the curly-haired man.

"No rugs," says the boy. Then, as if he were obligated to offer *some* information, he adds: "She likes wood." His face flushes slightly as he says this.

"Me too," says the curly-haired man. He looks at his partner, who is pulling his gloves again. "You like wood, Ellis?"

"Right now I don't like anything but the beer I ain't drinking," the man says with a grin. "So let's get the stuff in and hit that bar across the street." He looks at the boy. "It's a good bar. She's a lucky lady to live so close."

"You can't live anywhere and not live close to a bar," says the boy quickly. "They're everywhere."

"Not good ones," says the man. "Not like that one over there. She's lucky to live close to a *good* one." He glances at the front wall. "Weird, ain't it? She don't have a view of the street. Too bad. I never saw a room like this without a front window looking out on the street. Must have been a closet there or something. Tore it out and made a room to rent. This place is old." He looks back at the boy as he shuffles toward the door. "Bud, you must have been pretty desperate to take a place with no window looking out on the action."

"Pretty desperate," the boy says. "Let's get the stuff in. Then you can go."

*   *   *

"Can *some*one help me with stockings?" says a large woman with short black hair. She is waving a plastic leg fitted with a dark brown mesh; the end of the mesh flaps off the abruptly chopped thigh.

From the back of the shop a tall, elegant woman dressed in green walks calmly toward the plastic leg. "What may I find for you, Harriet?" she says, with a cool smile.

The woman with the leg stops waggling it. "Oh. Hello, Louise."

"Hello, nice to see you. May I take that?"

"Sure."

The woman in green places the leg on its toe above a display of scarves. It stands. The large woman says, "Sorry. I get kind of carried away in here when no one comes."

"Not at all," says the woman in green smoothly. "I understand. I'm sorry you had to wait."

"It's all right. It's worth it." She looks around the store as they walk down an aisle. "Things have really picked up for you."

The woman in green makes a modest nod as she pulls several cellophane envelopes from a cubbyhole. She spreads them on top of a sweater rack for the large woman to see. "They *have* picked up—thanks to you and our other friends. It's remarkable." She laughs. "We must be doing something right, entirely by luck." She gestures toward the stockings and says softly, "This shade looks very *trim* with the prints I know you like."

The large woman picks out three of the envelopes. "Hardly luck. Such wonderful taste." She hands over the packets. "I'll take these." As they walk to the front counter together, she adds, "But really, Louise—have you thought about getting some more help?"

"Well, dear, I have. And as a matter of fact, we are." Louise stops, and looks at the large woman for a moment. "I hope it works out."

The woman looks puzzled. "Why shouldn't it? It's a small enough shop—surely someone can learn easily."

Louise nods distractedly. She looks at the woman for another moment, and says, "It's rather an experiment, though."

"I suppose it always is. New personality, unknown skills—kind of a challenge."

Louise thinks, seeming not to hear. Then she says, "Yes, no doubt. Well, here, dear—Lynn will take care of you. Thanks for coming by, and I hope the wait—"

She breaks off as the front door opens and the boy steps into the shop. He looks at her and removes his wool cap; she nods and gestures toward the rear of the store. They walk back down separate aisles and meet in a small office.

"Sorry to bother you at such a busy time," the boy says.

She dismisses this with a nod. "What can I do for you?"

"Well—first, I just wanted to . . ." He shrugs. "To make sure everything is still . . . smooth. That you're still expecting her the day after tomorrow."

"Of course," says Louise. He waits. She says, "As for smooth, well—I suppose. I *hope.*" She studies him, and smiles. "Frankly, I think you're in a better position than I am, as far as assuring smoothness. You know her, and"—she lets go a little laugh— "could probably assure *me*—"

He sighs sharply. "She's an alcoholic. I've . . . We've discussed this before; I can't assure you of anything. Nobody can assure you of anything with an alcoholic." He frowns. She looks mildly alarmed at his earnestness; he tries to lighten it by adding,

"You can ask anyone. I mean, everyone in the world knows this, now."

She exhales a deep breath. "Yes. I suppose everyone does. I suppose it's amazing, if you think of it, that with a staff of six, and the usual turnover, I have never *had* one here. I mean, when you consider that practically half of the population is . . . that way, well, it's simply amazing—"

"It is," he says. "And it's sixty-nine percent."

"What?"

"Of the adult population. Sixty-nine percent are alcoholics. You're probably thinking of the number in treatment: *that's* the fifty-percent figure. Or close—it's more like forty-eight percent now. It dropped in the last quarter, which isn't good, actually. . . ." He frowns suddenly and stops with a flush. She gapes at him.

"Sorry," he says. "I kind of run on sometimes."

"No, please," she says hastily. She puts out a hand, but quickly withdraws it. His awkwardness is passing without her. She says, "Yes, well—I'm really quite . . . quite *pleased* to be, to have the opportunity to help someone with—with this affliction. I mean"—she laughs again—"I guess I've practically been living in the twentieth century! Now my little shop will have the chance to catch up, really—to be more a part of our times, when all of us should take a hand in the fight against this terrible, terrible—"

"And there's the tax break," he says, holding out a manila envelope. "That's nice, too."

She stops short and blushes, and seems about to snap at him. But instead she takes the envelope, opens it with a cool motion, and quickly reads the form inside. Her expression changes from anger to wonder.

"How did you get this?" she says. "This—to tell you the truth, I didn't . . . well, *believe* it when you told me about it. And I certainly never thought anything would actually be processed—"

"It's the law," he says. "It's a good law."

"Yes, but—the government!" She laughs with raised eyebrows. "The government takes ten months even to cash a tax *check*. To get an exemption processed in less than a week . . ." She looks at the form again. "It's amazing."

He says nothing. She looks up from the form at him. After a moment she says, "Or, I think, perhaps it's that *you're* amazing." This time she puts her hand out all the way, and touches his arm. "You are quite a young man. I hope your mother appreciates all that you're doing. You've bought her such a stylish collection of clothes, you've gotten her an apartment, a job—"

"Thank you," he says, putting his cap back on

with the arm she touches. He smiles thinly, and rather brusquely shakes the hand she still extends. Then he turns and leaves the office.

She stands, her hand still slightly in front of her, staring at the doorway. She sighs, frowns, and says, "Well, by God—" At that moment he sticks his head back in the doorway.

"Hi," he says, with a brief smile. She stares. "One thing," he says. He frowns slightly, looks at the floor, then meets her eyes.

"What is it?" she says.

He nods. "My mother will be here the day after tomorrow, to *work*. I mean—she's not . . . you know, a sort of symbol of the times, or anything. She's a smart person who will need a job and can do it. Pardon me for mentioning it. Thank you. Good-bye." He is gone.

"Not at all," says the woman. "Not at all."

MONDAY

T H R E E

She's done well here, you know—*very* well," says the thin man in the white coat, staring hard across his desk at the boy and pulling on one end of a mustache so pale it is nearly transparent. "One of the best turnarounds in *years*, probably. We are justifiably proud of it."

The boy says softly, with what seems to be more approval than irony, "Yes, she's very good at turnarounds."

The man stiffens his stare, and moves his hand to

let his mouth show the beginning of a knowing smile—nearly a sneer. "Oh, I see. Irony, is it?"

"No, really," says the boy, but the man talks right through him.

"Feeling good and bitter. Ready to let her have it, get even, score on old accounts once you get her back where you can work on her." The man nods sharply, points a finger. The boy closes his mouth and looks off to a corner of the room. "Well, don't be too sure. We make them stronger than you think—and we're wise to the vengeful nature of families. Our clients are vulnerable when they are taken home, certainly, but they don't crumple. You can count on that."

"I *do*," says the boy. But the man isn't finished.

"We spend a week of every month teaching them how to withstand it," he says. "One fourth of the time. That's a lot, but it's necessary: Families are merciless." He drops his finger, crosses his arms, sits back. "We call it *recrimination.*" He speaks the word as if he and his colleagues created it from scratch.

They sit for a few moments, the man jiggling fingers against his arms, the boy clearly deciding if he should respond.

"I can't pretend I won't feel some bitterness," he says carefully. "Sure. But"—he glances at the man, then back to the corner of the room—"I've gotten over it before. I've gotten very good at controlling it. And . . . after all, she *is* my mother. I mean, there are bigger feelings than resentment."

"You're damn right you can't pretend you won't feel it," says the man. He uncrosses his arms, leans forward, and looks down at the file open on his desk. The boy says nothing and stares into the corner, occasionally glancing at the man, who flips pages curtly. After a few minutes the man shakes his head, tapping an index fingernail in rapid irritation on his desk.

He sighs loudly. "To your custody alone." He shakes his head again.

"Yes," says the boy. He hesitates, then adds: "I *am* fourteen."

The man grunts without looking up. "A lot of people dislike that law."

"The law says *thirteen* is enough," the boy says.

The man says drily, "As you might imagine, I'm quite aware that thirteen is 'enough.' According to the law."

"I don't suppose you argue with the law that says twelve is enough to refer a parent for committal."

Deliberately, the man frowns at the file, closes it, and looks across the desk at the boy. "Yes. So, tell me, then—why is it that you waited six months, until you had reached the ripe old age of twelve-and-a-half, to commit your mother to our care?"

The boy blinks twice. "I wanted to see if it could work out at home."

"Ah, but according to your affidavit of committal"—he taps the file—"it had already *not* been working out for two years. I would think you'd have been eagerly waiting for that manly twelfth birthday so you could stow your mother away and solve the problems of the world all by yourself. Why wait?"

The boy swallows. His expression does not change—it is simple in its polite openness—but his coloring does: He goes slightly more pale with each comment from the man across the desk. When he speaks, his voice stays polite, but its tone is thinned. "I was never 'waiting' to commit her. When the time for committal came, it was not because I had reached a certain *birthday*—it was because things were going badly." He stops, then adds: "I wasn't doing a good job with things." He stops once more, but adds: "I did not like to do it. I did not like bringing her here. It was . . ." He sighs.

"Thank you very much," the man says with mock brightness. "Then why, when you reached the even riper old age of thirteen, did you hesitate to liberate her? The minimum commitment, as a legal scholar like you must know, is only six months or until the thirteenth birthday of the child with custody." He holds his hands, palms up, toward the boy. "There you are, child with custody. Here your mother is, locked in this"—he loudly imitates the boy's sigh—"place. Why not spring her as soon as you could?"

The boy sits still for several seconds. During these moments his good color returns; when he speaks, his voice is full again. He looks the man in the eyes. "Please finish your verification of my family's papers," he says quietly.

"Oh, I see. And keep my technically unauthorized questions to myself?"

The boy smiles. "Right," he says.

The man holds the boy's stare for a moment. He opens the file again, clears his throat, and says, "What about the other child?"

"Excuse me?"

"The brother. It says there's a brother."

"He's . . . in second-term custody," the boy says. He pulls some papers from a large envelope in his lap, and holds them across the desk. His face is flushed; he speaks more rapidly than before. "He attends an undoctrinated private school, and he lives with—"

"So I've read," the man says, ignoring the extended papers. He studies the boy. Then he smiles.

The boy, still flushed, looks quickly to the side, then back at the man; finally, with a wrinkle between his eyes, he returns part of the smile.

"You've done a very nice job," the man says.

"Of . . . ?"

"You've done a very nice job. Of separating him from the trouble with your mom. With his mom."

The boy watches him; after a moment he nods cautiously.

The man returns the nod. He smiles again. The boy watches. The man says, "What I want to know is one thing."

The boy does not move.

"What I want to know," says the man, patting the file, "is how this neatly sanitized kid is going to take the sudden appearance in his life of an alcoholic mother." He makes a helpless gesture with his hands. "This kid probably hasn't even had AO. You've probably protected him even from that."

"His school—"

"Sure," says the man. "Probably why you picked it. And his fosters—they look very cute as well."

The boy takes several seconds. "Yes," he says. He takes a short, deep breath. "Yes, they are. They have a good house, a lot of generosity, they look nice and speak nicely to each other and my brother and probably everybody else in the world. They are intelligent. They are flexible. Plus, they are sober. Extra plus, they are sober *not* because they go to a church that makes them superior and afraid, but because they're smart and don't have it in their blood. Cute? You bet. They are *adorable.* "

The man smiles at the speech. "Well, then," he says, "one more time: How is your brother going to handle an alcoholic mom all of a sudden?"

The boy doesn't answer. The man takes a package of cigarettes from a drawer and lights one. He winces at the first inhalation, and blows the smoke away from the boy with exaggerated courtesy. "So how about the kid? And how about *you?*" he says. "How are *you* going to handle her? Because you haven't seen this one yet, Mister Fourteen. She's going to come out of here all clean and soft, but don't get your hopes up. Within a few weeks—maybe even a few days—she may be drunk again, drunk and puking in the kitchen or kissing ugly men in the bars or hitting you or whatever it was she did that drove you to commit her." He takes another drag on his cigarette. "How're you going to handle this woman?"

The boy says, "I'm not going to 'handle' her. She's going to handle herself. And I'm going to handle myself. *The alcoholic is never sober by the acts of others*—remember?"

"Look who's quoting AO," says the man, raising his eyebrows. The boy looks down. "Yes," the man continues, "you get an A plus. As I see from your records. But what does your brother get? Can he handle *him*self? Or—" The man stops, leans forward and points at the boy. "You probably *would* try it! You're planning on keeping them apart. Not letting them meet. Not even *telling* him." He watches the boy, who raises his eyes but says nothing. The man nods, and laughs. "You *would*, you sharpie. Oh, watch yourself, Mister Fourteen. Deep waters here."

"I know the law," the boy says.

"Yes. But this *is* the boy's *mother*. And there are bigger obligations than legality, yes?"

The boy stands up and holds out his hand. "My papers are in order." It is not a question.

The man folds the file with gestures of extreme courtesy. "Indeed, sir." He hands it across the desk.

The boy takes it. "The release is scheduled for tomorrow."

The man bows his head.

"Then we don't need to talk again." The boy turns to go.

"Just leave everything to you, eh?"

The boy turns back. The man is grinning. The boy says, "If you want to put it that way."

"The Alcoholic Offspring cherish the illusion of control over all lives that touch them," says the man.

"My mother's life is not an illusion," says the boy.

The man laughs. "You're a tough one, aren't you?"

The boy stands straight. "Yes," he says. "Yes. Sometimes people *are,* you know."

"Sure, kid. I hope Oliver's tough too."

The boy waits. "What about my mother? Any hopes for her?"

The man waves a hand. "The last thing she needs is hope. *She'll* be all right. Drunks are tough. It's the rest of us who need to be careful."

The boy leaves.

F O U R

The streets of northeast Washington are quiet in winter. Three-story row houses, many with cupolas or other old, fancy features, line up along narrow roads unshaded by leafless trees but dark nonetheless, because it is late on a gray afternoon. Yellow lights show within a few houses. Most are dark within.

The boy, Sam, is sitting at the end of one street, on a small hill looking over an old field that used to be a parking lot; patches of ragged macadam jut above its flatness. A vacant factory of flesh-colored brick stands in the middle of the field. One of its outside walls is crumbling. All of its windows are broken. Past the factory, the field and the patches stretch for half a mile; beyond are the tops of more row houses in the distance, most of them dark.

Sam is not alone. Beneath him on the hill, about fifty feet away, sits an old man in a puffy red wool coat. The coat is old too, but not as old as he is. Like Sam, he stares across the field as if there were something to see besides a barren factory. He was there when Sam arrived, and he has not looked around at the boy. He suddenly speaks, but in an easy tone of conversation.

"Ever wonder why somebody built so damn many little houses squinched together like that?" He turns and gives Sam a look with his eyebrows raised. It seems like a look of welcome—to the spot, and to the information offered. The man is black. His curly white hair encloses his round face like a light from behind.

Sam feels obligated to twist and look behind him at the houses. "No," he says.

The old man is looking at the field again. "This was a boom town once. But not a boom town like you read about in history books—didn't have the big feature, like gold around Denver, sunshine around Los Angeles, chip firms around Chapel Hill. Didn't have a *draw.*" He looks back at Sam. "Washington got big because it was on the way to somewhere else."

"Baltimore?" says Sam, uncertainly.

The man chuckles. "Nope. It was New York. People used to be crazy to get to New York. People from the South. Black people, especially. You know anything about the Civil War?" He turns and fixes Sam with an appraising look.

"Well . . . a little," the boy says hesitantly.

The man sighs, and looks back to the field. "A little. I reckon that's all I can expect, even from a *smart* boy. And you're a smart boy, I can tell." He nods. "Well, it wasn't a little *war.* We don't have wars anymore so you got no way of comparing, but we studied them when I was a boy and believe me— it was the biggest America ever had. And when it was over, lots of black people in the South suddenly had places to go. Places up North. Places like New York, with the big fun and all the money waiting to be paid to good working folks. This is a long time ago, I'm talking." He hums for a few seconds. Sam just sits. "Only it was a hard road to get to New York from Georgia and Carolina. And when you're getting tired and the traveling money's gone, and you hit a nice town like D.C., well—suddenly it seems big *enough*, even if it ain't the biggest. The lights shine pretty bright at night, even if there ain't quite as many. And there's lots more room to find yourself a spot." He turns and gestures behind them. "There's a mess of spots back there."

"I see," says Sam.

"This is a *long* time ago, now."

"Yes," says Sam.

The man hums some more. Sam watches the field. After a while the man says, "You know what they used to make in that factory?"

Sam thinks. "Probably CRTs."

"Right," says the man. "Just what they used to make in most *all* the closed-down factories you see around now." He hums. "They figure the cathode-ray tube is why two out of every five houses on these streets are empty. No babies."

"I know," says Sam.

The man shakes his head. "Didn't take but fifty years for them to figure it out, did it? Boy, they're sharp. Just a couple of generations, televisions on fourteen hours a day, kids sitting in front of computers all day at school and all night at home, birthrate going down fifty to sixty percent when they grow up, just half a century of this and our geniuses figured it out. That's science. *Fast.*"

Sam says nothing. The man watches the factory, then says, "People won't even go in the places now.

Afraid they'll catch something." He laughs and shakes his head. "Stupid without fear one minute, stupid with too much the next."

"Would you go in there?" asks Sam.

The man turns and looks at him. "Why, yes," he says, with a nod. "Yes, I would. Matter of fact, I used to go in there quite a bit before the tube crash. I worked in there."

"In there?" Sam points. The man nods. "Doing what?"

"Assembly."

"Assembly," Sam repeats. Then he says, "Do *you* have any children?"

The man smiles. "Six."

"Six!" The boy gapes.

"And I *touched* the tubes. *Thousands* of them, every day."

"But they weren't switched on," Sam says. "It was the radiation from the cathode rays that made people sterile. When they were *on*. Of course they didn't hurt you."

The man nods. "I told you you were a smart boy. I'll tell you something else, too. It wasn't just the tubes made people stop having the babies. They blame the tubes, but they're just part of it."

"I know," Sam says.

"The Juice," says the man. "The Juice has got to take the blame, too."

"I know," Sam says.

"They're just *beginning* to get to the bottom of the bottle on this alcohol thing, and their big Epidemic was declared officially over five years ago. Epidemic—shoo!" He makes a sardonic laugh. "Just a word so they could say it was under control. Can't control it unless you name it."

He looks up at Sam. "Your parents alcoholics, son?"

"My mother," says Sam.

"What about your daddy?"

"He's gone."

"Dead?"

"No. Just gone."

The man grunts. "She at home?"

"No," says the boy.

"At a center, then. Which one? Soberlife?"

Sam nods.

"They're the cleverest ones," the man says. "I've had four kids in Soberlife, two in Richmond, one in San Francisco, one in Ann Arbor. The Soberlife people played it smart. Let a few small go-getters start the early centers and mess up because of the volume. Then step in, buy them out, and demand government regulation. Which means government *funding*. Man. You know Soberlife is now the second-biggest organization in this country, after the postal service? With the armed forces nearly out of business, it's bigger than the *government.*"

"Yes," says Sam. "They like to tell you that."

"I bet they do. I read it in the paper, but I bet they talk about it a lot when they take your family in, and begin collecting that money per drunk per day. Like being big means they don't mess up."

"They say they have a lot of experience," says Sam. After a moment he says, "I think they have too much, maybe."

The man nods. "Right. See it every day and it ain't your family, it stops hurting."

Sam watches the field. Off on the far edge, a small gang of children appears, running toward the factory. Sam says, "Something you said confuses me."

"I hate to confuse people," says the man. "Do me a favor and ask."

"You said you had four kids in Soberlife. But you said, 'I bet they do,' when I said the Soberlife counselors like to brag about the size. You said it as if they didn't say it to *you.*"

"They didn't," says the man. "They never said a word to me, because I've never been within a mile of a Soberlife."

"Then . . . you didn't commit your kids?"

"Nope." The man stares out over the field.

The boy watches him. "Who did?"

"I would personally never commit a person to a place like that," says the man. "They call it an institution." He makes a shallow laugh. "I told them what I believe. I personally believe the *family* is the institution. I told the kids. It's the place to solve the problems. I'm talking about *me*, here. Maybe I'm wrong. The kids thought I was. They believed in *science.*"

"Who committed them?" the boy insists.

The old man sits quietly. "Their children," he says. "The kids."

The gang on the field has disappeared behind the factory. The boy and the man watch for several minutes. The gang appears around the near corner, seven or eight boys, running. Sam says, "Did it work?"

"What?" says the man. "Did what work?"

"Science," says Sam.

The old man says, "Two of them are drunk today. One's a Steemer. The fourth is dead." He takes a big breath, lets it out, and shrugs. "One out of four sober and the one don't really count, because Steemers ain't hardly human. Who knows? Maybe the family wouldn't have done any better.

And nobody pays you per drunk per day in the family. Ain't no science, either. You got to make it up as you go."

Sam starts to say something, but suddenly he stands up, staring at the gang of boys. They are closer now, running in a pack, weaving across the field. Their voices are just audible, high laughs and hollers. Sam stares. The old man turns to see what has happened to him, then looks back at the gang. Sam's face breaks from tense concentration into a bright grin. He waves an arm and shouts: "Ollie!"

The pack of boys breaks stride for an instant; heads swing toward Sam, then toward one boy who has stopped altogether. A few whistles and laughs pierce the air; the pack moves on. One boy is left, looking after them, back at Sam, after them, back at Sam, after them. They move on. The boy begins to walk toward the hill.

Sam calls out to the old man, "My brother. My kid brother, Oliver." Then he runs down the hill.

The man raises a hand, without turning around.

The boys meet on a disk of macadam. "Hi," says Ollie, with a little wave, when they are still fifteen feet apart. He stops.

Sam bounds right up to him. "Hey, man!" He is grinning, panting from his run, jouncing on the balls of his feet. His arms don't know what to do—they move in choppy gestures and hesitations. His breath keeps appearing and vanishing between them. He grins hard. "Hey, Ollie."

"Hi, Sam," says Ollie, squinting slightly as he looks up. Sam notices the squint, and moves so the low sun is not behind him. Ollie still squints.

Sam says, "What a surprise, huh?"

"Yeah," says Ollie. He nods, and smiles a quick one. Then he says, "Were you, like, waiting for me or something?"

"No," says Sam. "It's a *surprise*. Pretty neat, huh? I'm just sitting there, listening to this geeze from the twentieth century talk about the *Civil War*, Ol, if you can feature that. He's so old you could almost believe he fought in it, man. So he's going on and on, and I look up, and—whammo!—there's my brother running across the field with his street gang, on their way to hold up a grocery store."

Ollie looks quickly at Sam. "I wouldn't do that."

"Oh, I'm just kidding," says Sam. "Who are they, your soccer team?" He begins walking leisurely in the direction the boys took.

"Yeah," says Ollie, following. "My soccer team."

"Coming from practice or something?"

"Yeah," says Ollie. Then: "Well, not real practice. We practice at night, remember? At the indoor field."

"Right," says Sam. "Sure."

"This was more of, like, a pickup game. Kind of a practice game or something."

"You still the goalie?"

"What? Oh. Yeah."

Sam nods. "But don't you ever . . ." He skips a couple of steps, gesturing with his arms, then leaps into a sudden soccer kick at a chunk of tar, leg slicing from behind him and through the air in a quick arc, his foot missing the tar by an inch. "Don't you ever want to carry the ball, fake a defender, drop a pass, pick it back up . . . and *score*?"

Ollie says, "Wow. That was a nice kick, Sam. You could probably kick pretty good."

"Pretty *well*," says Sam. Walking again, he puts his hands in his pockets, shrugs his shoulders, laughs once. "Yeah. I could kick. I don't know." He shrugs and laughs again.

"You ought to play," says Ollie. "I mean, it'd be easier if you were in school, but there's leagues that play at night. I bet your boss would sponsor a team or something."

"Oh, yes," says Sam. "An industrial-league soccer team from a two-man printshop. In goal, a sixty-year-old ninety-pound reformed alcoholic with a glass eye; on offense, a fourteen-year-old ninety-three-pound typesetter who looks great kicking air. I bet the teams from the taverns would line up to play us."

"Well," says Ollie. He shrugs. "You could play something, somewhere, if you looked."

"I'm not much on the team sports," says Sam. Then he turns toward Ollie, smiles, and cuffs him on the shoulder. "Not like my brother the star here. You still playing in the concert band too? *That's* a team sport if ever there was one."

"Yeah," says Ollie, taking the cuff. "Sure is."

"Where's the horn?"

"At home. We don't rehearse at school. You know. We have rehearsals at night."

"Right. So when are we going to get a little recital? I know the Bigelows are too polite to ask, but I'm not. We'd all like to hear a few toots. How about a concert?"

"Oh, you know," says Ollie, looking down and hiking his shoulders. "I don't want to show you guys until I'm decent. I'm nervous. You know."

"Nervous," says Sam, lifting his hands in front of him. "Ladies and gentlemen, the guy says he's nervous. Too nervous to allow his blood brother, who toils all day in a grimy den of ink and clanking type, to watch a soccer practice, even from a distance, even though it takes place in the evening hours when the poor brother could attend."

"You promised," says Ollie quickly.

"Too nervous," Sam continues, "to allow his noble foster parents, who have gone to great expense to buy him a saxophone of the alto variety, to hear him play so much as a quick run through the main theme of the Jesse Jackson Early School's fight song."

"We don't really have, like, a fight song," says Ollie.

Sam laughs, and looks at Ollie again. "Nervous. A pulse rate of fifty-five, this guy has—the pulse rate of a great blue whale. Sturdy legs, with an inseam of twenty-two inches, that never jiggle in tension. Eyes that do not shift. A stomach that does not seize up in protest, even when he astounds it with seven ham biscuits washed down with root beer followed by two cream pies. Is this the metabolism, the diet of a nervous man?"

"The pies thing was last year," says Ollie. "You guys won't ever let that go away. And whales are extinct." He shakes his head. "Look, I just don't like to do anything in front of . . . people I know."

Sam puts his arm around the boy's shoulders. "Don't sweat it," he says. "I'm only teasing you." He looks suddenly concerned, and scrutinizes Ollie's head. "Hey, speaking of sweat—didn't you shower after your game?"

"Huh? Shower?"

"You should always let your muscles relax in a shower, and wash off the dried perspiration," says Sam. "We've been over this before. Why didn't you shower? I said you could play sports only if you took care of yourself."

"It was just a pickup game," says Ollie. "On, like, a *field*. It wasn't at the arena or anything. I mean, there were no showers. We just *played*." He looks quickly in the direction his friends have gone in. "We were playing."

Sam watches him, and follows the look. He nods. "Okay," he says. "But wear a cap next time. It's winter. Your head perspires and the pores open up, and hair doesn't really insulate very well." Ollie nods, and looks again in the direction of the gang.

Sam claps him on the shoulder. "Listen," he says, "I've got some things to do. Think you could catch up to your friends?"

"Sure," says Ollie, taking his hands out of his pockets. "Sure I could."

"Better get after them, then. I'll drop by tonight or tomorrow."

"All right," says Ollie. He bounces slightly on his legs, hesitating, looking at Sam. "So, I'll see you later?" Sam smiles and nods. Ollie says, "I mean, like, it's okay to go?"

"Sure," says Sam.

Ollie runs. Sam watches him sprint across the field, grow smaller and smaller, and disappear over a far ridge. It takes very little time.

He stands for a moment, then turns and walks back the way he came. After a few moments he looks up. The hill he sat on earlier is empty. The old man is gone.

F I V E

The voices from the living room stop as Ollie steps into the doorway. The man and woman look up at him.

"Bye," says Ollie, with a small wave. He holds up a small bag with the name of an athletic-shoe manufacturer on it. "Soccer."

The woman nods and says, "Oh. Of course," but the man frowns. "I thought it was band tonight," he says. "Monday was band, wasn't it?"

Ollie misses the slightest beat, then says, "Special practice for goalies. Coach got me out of band for it."

He looks at the floor and sighs. "I let in a few goals in the last scrimmage. More than a few."

"Hey, if you don't let a few in now and then, they start to take you for granted," says the man. "Don't get discouraged. You're still the first goalie, aren't you?"

Ollie nods reluctantly.

"Well, there you go," says the man. "You let the coach do the fretting. He knows a couple of goals don't mean anything but a lapse of concentration. You're his first choice: If he has faith in you, you should too." He looks at his wife. She smiles at the boy.

"Well," says Ollie, mustering a smile, "thanks. I guess you're right. Well. Okay. I got my bus fare. I'll be home the usual. Thanks."

Just as he is going, the woman says, "You're sure you're safe, Ollie?" She looks at her husband, then at the boy. "You go out so *much*. I just can't get used to it. A ten-year-old on the city buses. On the city *streets*."

" 'The city streets' . . . He's taking *one* bus down *one* street, ten blocks," the man says. "It's nearly door to door. He'll be fine." He looks at Ollie and winks. "Used to be a lot of crime in the streets at night, Oliver. Real wild times."

"Right," says Ollie. "I read about it in sociology." He looks at the woman. "I'll be fine, Mom."

The woman looks up sharply, her eyes full. After a second she manages to say, "Fine, Ollie." It is nearly a whisper.

Ollie is out the door.

Outside it is cold; he fastens the neck snap of his parka, gets his bus change into his palm, and slips his mittens on. He walks half a block to the bus stop.

The bus arrives. Ollie shucks his mitten, dumps the warm coins into the hopper, and takes a seat. But he does not get off in ten blocks. He rides several miles, deep into the city; when he does leave this bus, it is only to take another. After a second long ride, which takes him through streets that are dark but busy with vague shapes of silent people, he gets off and stands on a corner near a streetlight. He is seen by a beggar, who advances to the edge of the light's pool.

"What's in the bag, boy?"

Ollie unzips it, and shakes out wads of newspaper. He grins, as if expecting the man to curse in disappointment. Instead, the man chases the balls of paper as they blow in the cold wind. Ollie watches him catch one, flatten it with his feet, holding his hands up under his armpits—and then quickly stuff it inside his shirt with obviously stiff fingers. He chases another, out of sight in the dark.

Ollie shrugs, crumples his cloth bag, and stuffs it into his parka pocket. Then he leaves the light and slips around a corner down a street of irregular two- and three-story buildings that seem to lean toward one another at their tops. Most have no lights inside. He passes a small grocery, crossing the street before he reaches it and staying out of the light it casts on the sidewalk. A man is inside the door counting change from his hand into the grocer's; between them on the counter is a large turnip.

Suddenly the street divides. The main section continues around a cluster of buildings, passing in front of them; a very narrow road slips off behind the buildings. Ollie takes this way.

In a few moments he stops. He is at the back of a small stone building, with a door above six wooden steps. He watches the door. It, like the doors around it, is completely dark.

Ollie watches the door. Minutes pass. He pulls the cloth bag from his pocket, flattens it out, and stuffs it inside his parka across his chest. He begins to bounce on his legs.

Then, gradually, a light begins to appear through the cracks around the door. It is a mean little light, but soon it is undeniable: Someone is on the other side. Still Ollie waits, but now he no longer bounces. He takes a step forward, and pauses.

The door swings open. A candle appears around the edge. Ollie exhales a breath held for a long time, and walks toward it, and in. It closes. The light fades.

TUESDAY

S I X

The burgundy door opens. Through it steps
Sam. He looks around the room quickly: at
the trim bed with the early-twentieth-cen-
tury quilt, the small matching pine tables with draw-
ers, the two wicker chairs near the back window, the
three plain, bright floor lamps. Then he steps aside.
A moment later a young woman walks casually into
the room.

Once she is a few feet inside the door she stands still
and looks around. Her eyes don't linger—she sees
everything once, in turn, and then smiles at the boy.

"Thanks, Sambo," she says. "It's a neat place. Just put my luggage over there."

He smiles; neither of them is carrying any luggage. She moves to the front wall, puts her hands in the pockets of her raincoat, and sighs contentedly. "Love the view of that tavern across the street," she says. She looks back over her shoulder. "You're always thinking, Sam."

"Decent rooms are hard to come by," the boy says, with a slight frown. "They . . . you have to . . . I just took the first one that seemed—"

She laughs. It is a very natural laugh, high and strong, with no mockery. "Okay. Relax. I do like it. Two windows are plenty, and it doesn't matter which walls they're in."

Sam nods, and closes the burgundy door. The woman walks to the back window, glances out as she takes off her coat, then opens the closet and hangs it up. She gestures for Sam's coat, and while he is removing it, she passes her eyes over the garments hanging in the closet—perhaps six dresses, four blouses, a couple of sweaters and pairs of slacks. Sam hands her his coat. She looks him in the eye, and smiles. "When did my little boy learn how to buy pretty things for a woman?"

He shrugs, looks briefly into the closet and away. "Every little boy has a woman for a mother."

"Sure," she says. "And every little boy knows his mother's sizes, style, fabric preferences, and accessory needs, even when she's been in the slammer for a year and a half." She closes the closet door. As they turn back into the room, she says, "I can tell I'm going to get tired of saying 'Thanks.'"

"Then don't say it," Sam says.

She pretends to flop into one of the wicker chairs; really, it is more of a graceful descent with a flapping motion of the arms added at the end. He sits in the other. They look at each other. "We'll be all right," she says.

He studies her, raises his eyebrows noncommittally, smiles with pressed lips. She watches the expression; he holds it. She rolls her eyes, puts her head back, and laughs.

"God," she says, "you've mastered it. Even in my absence. Even without the primary stimulus. You've kept up your studies and progressed beautifully—far, I'm sure, beyond the dreams of the grand master who took you up as a prodigy and guided your early efforts. I refer of course to your father. God, I can't believe it."

"What," he says evenly, "are you talking about?"

"Priggishness," she says. "That expression, with the tight lips and the cool authority—it was the work of a man with the answers, a man in command, a man with patience for the weak and silence for the strong, a man full of levelheaded benefaction: in short, a prig." She leans forward and puts a hand on his knee. "Don't get me wrong. You can't help it. Your father passed on the genius, and I draw it out, like salt on sliced eggplant. All the same, I'm impressed with your progress."

He looks at her, sighs, and gets up.

"Where are you going?" she says.

"Your escape from 'the slammer' shouldn't be ruined by prigs," he says, standing by the chair. "I'll leave."

"Perfect!" She laughs and claps twice. "Sulking is, of course, the second stage of prigmanship. Hey." She stands up, puts her arms around him, and hugs him to her. "Come on. Don't let me sting you so easily. I'm just checking things out. If we're going to try this, we've got to try it for real."

" 'For real,' " he says. "You sound like a kid."

"And, as noted, you sound like a forty-two-year-old who sells life insurance. But who cares? Maybe a good mom lets her fourteen-year-old get away with sounding like a forty-two-year-old insurance sales-man. Maybe I'll learn. Let's go eat."

"I don't *want* to 'get away' with anything," he says, with a frown. With her arms still around him, she studies his face, smiling as he looks at her grimly.

"No," she says, pulling him softly into another hug, his head face out against her shoulder. "Of course not. Of course not." She holds him. After a moment she takes a deep breath, closes her eyes, and relaxes into a smile of private sweetness. "My big guy," she says.

But just as she does, Sam suddenly pulls back and looks into her face, with an excited grin. She looks startled. He is beaming. "What is it?" she says.

"You're being very sweet and polite," he says, "and I appreciate it. But I *know* what you must be going *crazy* to do!"

She shakes her head. "What—?"

He nods, grinning. "See *Ollie*!" He separates himself from her and heads for the closet. "Here I am keeping you to myself, but I just know . . ." His voice is muffled as he steps in to get their coats.

She watches his back, her forehead wrinkled, her eyes narrowed in concern.

S E V E N

The man in the black suit looks up from his reading in surprise as the heavy *clong* of a bell sounds through the halls between his office and the distant door. He utters a small exclamation as he pulls himself upright by the arms of the deep, wine-velvet chair. A large black dog stretches on the stone hearth, its short fur catching glimmers from the firelight beyond.

"It was a young preacher's idea, Bishop," says the man. The dog, settling down, twitches its ears forward at its name, but otherwise makes no move to join the man in walking toward the room's high oak door. "Young preachers don't want to miss a caller, at any time. They want to *hear* that doorbell, even when they are tucked away with a good book."

The dog settles its head on its paws and closes its eyes. "We're not young preachers anymore, are we, Bishop?" sighs the man as he reaches the door and opens it. "Now we wish we hadn't wired the spare matins bell to the door buzzer."

The man leaves the room and turns into a wide hallway. He waves his hand in front of an electric eye, and the hall pops into light. At its end he takes another turn, and another long corridor is illuminated at his wave. Two more halls bring him to a broad entryway with a high, vaulted ceiling of stone. He flicks two switches. The first ignites gas torches set in sconces on the stone walls; the second flashes three spotlights onto the porch just visible through arch-shaped windows high in the thick wooden door.

The man slides back a small metal panel in the door and bends to put his eye to it. "My goodness," he says. He stands up and rubs his chin with a hand, sliding the panel back with the other. "My good gracious goodness." He thinks for a moment, then smiles. The smile runs its course, fades, and is replaced by another, of greater warmth and charm. With this in place, he opens the door.

"Jack!" he says.

"Your Grace," says a small man, stepping quickly into the entryway. He shudders, then smiles tightly. "Thank you. A cold night."

"Be warmed," says the other man, sweeping his hand toward the interior of the building as he closes the door with a thick double click. It is a gallant gesture. He tempers it with a wry smile: "Be warmed, Prior Marloe. It *is* prior, is it not?"

The smaller man, unbuttoning his thin raincoat, matches the smile. "I could say I am always *fore*-warmed, upon coming here," he says. "And, yes, it is prior. But 'Jack' will do."

"So it will," says the older man. "Come."

They walk back through the hallways, without speaking. When they enter the firelit study, the young man glances quickly around as he makes for the hearth. The dog springs to its feet and flaps its tail. "Hello, Bishop," says the man, scratching its head heartily.

The older man waits until Marloe has finished scratching the dog and has turned with a seemingly contented sigh. Then he says, "I have been meaning to call."

"Really?" says Marloe.

"Of course," says the cardinal.

There is a pause. "Of course the church would have been honored to receive Your Grace," Marloe says with a small bow. "Despite the fact that we have no electricity yet, and do everything by candlelight. Coming to greet you at the door with a candle in my hand would be nicely humbling for me, but might be downright eerie for you."

"Churches *are* eerie, even when they boast electric-eye spotlights," says the cardinal. Marloe smiles. The cardinal says, "I sincerely hope you have found a good response from the . . . constituency you anticipated."

"And that I have stuck to my foresworn restrictions, and have not started stealing your flock?" Marloe laughs sincerely.

The cardinal laughs as well. They watch each other.

"Well," says Marloe, walking toward a chair, "things have gone well enough. The group of people I hoped to reach are there, and they *are* responding." He arrives at the chair, but instead of sitting he turns, to look at the cardinal. "But I've reached something I had not anticipated. And I need to ask for your counsel."

The cardinal raises a hand; it is a noncommittal

gesture. Marloe nods, as if acknowledging its ambiguity, and continues. "I'm a little uncertain of how to talk about all of this with you. In view, I mean, of your . . . well, if not rejection, at least disapproval—"

"Come, come," says the cardinal, rather sharply. "Don't be melodramatic. I neither rejected nor disapproved. You left *me*, remember? I simply took the position—as titular leader of this church and, for better or worse, the person responsible for its service to society and God—that the worldly and spiritual rights of a certain group of children, defined by a capability I still fear is imaginary, were not the broadest base for a sound theological mission."

Marloe laughs curtly. "You were certainly more pointed than that."

"I was," says the cardinal, leaning forward. "I was indeed. And I could be more pointed still." The men lock eyes. After a few moments Marloe says, "You called me a young fool."

The cardinal sits back with a sigh. "I did, and it's a sin for which I will atone; if you never accept my apology, perhaps the Creator will, come Judgment Day."

"I've accepted your apology," says Marloe, looking down. "It's petty of me to mention it again. I'm sorry. Obviously, you struck some insecurity in myself with the name-calling."

"I would rather have struck you with the statistics on declining birthrates," the cardinal says drily. "They seem quite a bit more conducive to insecurity than a harsh word from an *old* fool." He shakes his head incredulously. "Such damning clarity: Even fifteen years after the tube crash, birthrate down eleven percent last year, from a nine percent drop the year before, from a fourteen percent drop the year before, from a twenty-two percent before that. And you want to go after *kids*! A church for kids! They are becoming as rare as guileless men used to be."

"I've heard the stats before, thank you," says Marloe.

But the cardinal is leaning forward and pointing. " 'Heard,' yes; but not 'believed.' "

"I believe my calling," says Marloe quietly.

"Calling! You believe your brilliant *ideas*," says the older man. "I grant you, they *are* brilliant—your angle on the children who look to themselves alone instead of to adults or God, your new compassion for their alcoholic parents, your pricking of gut fears about the kids' congenital doom—all very cogent. Everything—except your insistence that the world is full of these hyperresponsible youths, which as you know I seriously doubt—is very well plotted."

"You speak as if my calling were a graph," says Marloe. "But it isn't, and you know it. You know it's not as cold as that. And you're ignoring a big part of its inspiration—that someone has to offer a clean-breaking alternative to the disgraceful, exclusive smugness of the Steemer sects."

The cardinal says, "A church should not be formed to offer an alternative to other churches. It should be formed to offer an alternative to sin."

"Oh, stop it," snaps Marloe. "Just drop the anti-competition pretense altogether, please. Are you above worrying about the decline of your member-ship here—about eight percent last year, I recall; it was one of the first projects you put me on, remem-ber?—as the overall population grows more and more aligned with what the statisticians refer to as 'the church'? Almost ninety percent of the sober people in this city go to church four or more times a week. But they come *here* less and less. You are *losing* them. And you know who is taking them right out of your hands—and God's."

Marloe throws his arm out toward the street. "Those . . . *wild* men, with their violent judgmental-ism, their stupefying narrowness, their disdain for the weak and diseased—their extremely precise re-flection of what most of the scared people in the world want to believe. That only *they* are chosen for grace. That alcoholism is a God-sent curse striking only evil people. That sterility is a blessing to free us from the nagging of inferior beings—children—so that we may better pursue redemption through sanctified selfishness." He blows out a big breath. *"There is your enemy. That's* what people are leaving you for. And you won't face it. You prefer to play at *brotherhood* with the maniacs, a brotherhood of intolerance. What are you hoping for? A share of the booty they have already stolen from you?"

The cardinal is quiet for a time. Finally, he smiles gently. "Your oratory has improved wonderfully, prior. I envy the congregation that hears such phrases in the bosom of the church. 'Stupefying narrowness . . . violent judgmentalism . . . wild men . . . maniacs.' Nothing judgmental in *that*, of course." He sighs. "And I must say, your dazzling condemnation of our rivals—as you would have it—at First Church of Christ, Abstemious, is tempting to embrace."

"Yes?" says Marloe. He watches the cardinal. "So?"

The cardinal shrugs. He meets Marloe's eyes. "I was taught that temptations are to be suspected. And I suspect this one. You see, I have been fighting for *years* not to hate the Steemers. So many things about them are so offensive. Their aggressiveness. Their rigidity. Certainly, their lack of compassion for our poor alcoholic brethren. And their *confidence.*" He sighs again, heavily. "Yet I do not give myself the right to judge them. Or to dismiss them. Accommodation, you would say. Perhaps so. Yet I must count myself a servant of God among *men*. Among people. And a faith that claims a vast majority of the people I am among . . . well, I cannot set myself up as an antagonist. I cannot help doubting that I have the right."

Marloe nods. "Very humble," he says.

The cardinal groans and makes a gesture of dismissal. Marloe ignores it. "There's one point with regard to this 'vast majority' business," the young man says.

"I suppose I'm going to hear it."

"The 'vast majority' you claim for your Steemer brethren is nothing of the kind."

The cardinal laughs once. "I would have called ninety percent of the—"

"Of course you would. So would they. To them, the only people in the world worth having in church are the thirty-one percent of the population that is clean. *That's* what they have ninety percent of—and no matter what you and they cook up in the way of numbers, that's a minority. A special-interest group—a 'freak congregation,' if you'll allow me to borrow the term you used a month ago to damn my own plans."

"I have damned nothing."

"By condoning the Steemers you have practically damned sixty-nine percent of our people," says Marloe with grim force. He stares as he buttons his coat. Both men let the words die into silence. "Soon you'll be checking sobriety certification cards at the door on Sunday mornings," says Marloe as he bends to give the dog a last pat.

"Ah, Jack," says the cardinal, leaning back in his chair. "But you'll be right there among 'em, eh? Sleeves rolled up, taking the odd drink now and then to 'relate' to your flock, repeating your sermons on Wednesday nights so that those who were in a blackout on Sunday won't miss the wisdom . . ." He chuckles. "Had you been in the church two centuries ago, you'd have been on one of those boats to Africa, bearing pocket Bibles. And a hundred ninety-nine years ago you'd have been eaten in the jungle."

Marloe is at the door. "Good night, Your Grace. Thank you for the counsel."

"Ah! Yes! There was a problem to discuss. Wait!"

Marloe turns. The cardinal pulls himself to the edge of his chair. "Whatever our differences, Jack, I would like to help you."

Marloe considers. He shakes his head.

The cardinal nods. Then he smiles. "Come,

come—you don't want me sitting here making horrid assumptions that justify all of my doubts."

Marloe considers again, briefly. With a frown he says, "I have . . . reached someone who has responded with . . . an unexpected degree of fervor."

The cardinal claps his hands once and holds them together. "Why, Jack! You have an apostle! How marvelous—I haven't had one in forty-five years of priesthood, unless we count you. You are to be congratulated! So there *are* hapless mega-youths out there ready to look booze in the eye and shape a sunrise for the future. Grand! Where's the problem in *that*?"

Marloe watches the cardinal's performance. "The problem is that the boy's excitation doesn't have much to do with the teachings of our church. It's—bitter. Negative. It's aggressive, and directed entirely at alcoholics, like the Steemer line. I think my church was chosen just because it's new and has 'child' in its title."

The cardinal says, "So you have the chance now to steal back one of the many stolen from us. This is not a problem, prior. It is the chance to instruct. You are the one who wants to offer an 'alternative.' Very well—offer away! Demonstrate your new vision."

Marloe nods, buttons his collar, and stands on the edge of the hall's darkness. "Yes," he says. "But—he doesn't *listen.*" He looks for a long moment at the cardinal. "I cannot understand how a child can be clearheaded enough to seek help with such urgency, and yet be so inattentive to the help that's right in front of him. It's . . . it's just *perverse*!"

The cardinal nods. "Well, Father," he says. "You're the one who wanted a church full of children. Now you'll have to find a way to bring them to God."

"I hope they would listen to *Him*," Marloe says. And he steps into the darkness and walks away with footsteps that do not echo.

E I G H T

Sam looks up from a thick magazine with a photograph of a large printing plant on the cover. Someone has knocked on his door. He waits for a moment, listening. The knock comes again. Sam answers it.

It is Ollie. "Hi," he says, smiling briefly.

Sam blinks. After a second he smiles. "Ollie," he says. "Wow. A visit."

"Yeah," says Ollie. "Can I come in?"

Sam steps back, sweeps his arm inward. Ollie

walks past him straight to a chair and stands, looking inquisitively back at Sam.

"Sit down," says Sam. "Please."

Ollie nods and sits, looking around a limited area of floor and wall in front of him. "Nice place, Sam," he says.

"Thanks," says Sam automatically. Then he thinks for a moment. "My gosh, Ol—is this the first time you've been here?"

Ollie shrugs. Sam frowns. "I can't believe it," he says, still thinking. He shakes his head. "It *is* the first time. Jeez, Ollie. I'm *sorry*. It's . . . it's hard to believe—I mean, you know—"

"It's okay," says Ollie. He shrugs again. "What's the difference?"

But Sam goes on, urgent and fascinated. "It's just that it's so *weird*. I mean, well, I spend a lot of time thinking about you and stuff, more probably than you'd believe, and yet here I go and don't have you over for a *year*. . . ."

Ollie is looking at the floor. He says nothing. Sam gestures for another few moments, then sinks into a chair with a sigh. "Sorry," he repeats.

Ollie says, "I need you to let me do something."

Sam sits forward. "Sure," he says. "I mean, you know—"

"It's nothing bad."

"Of course it isn't," says Sam.

"The Bigelows want me to stop going to all my practices," says Ollie.

Sam says, "Ah. You want me to tell *them* to let you do something. Something that's between you and them." He sits back, watching Ollie.

Ollie nods. "They say I can't do soccer and band," he says. "They say it's too much. They don't want me out at night." He laughs suddenly, with bitterness. "They say they're *scared.*"

Sam is studying him. "They probably worry that you might run into trouble on the street. There used to be a lot of crime. Even violence. They probably remember. It's because they're thinking about your safety, Ol."

"Well, they can leave that to me," Ollie says. He flicks a glance at Sam. "And you, of course."

"How many nights a week do you go out?"

Ollie begins to jiggle a leg. "I don't know," he says. "It's different. Sometimes we have a lot of practice."

"Like how much? Three nights a week?"

"Three," says Ollie, "sometimes four. But so what? I mean, I'm doing good stuff." He looks at the floor for a moment. Then he looks at Sam. "I'm not behind in school, I'm not tired or sick or anything, I'm not almost getting murdered at the bus stop every night." He looks back at the floor. "I *got* to do my stuff, Sam. It's what I *like.*"

Sam says, "As opposed to what you don't like?"

Ollie says nothing.

"Is there so much in your life you don't like, Ol?" Sam is sitting forward again. "I mean, aside from this problem for a minute, is there a lot that makes you unhappy?"

Ollie glances at him. After a moment he says, "No. You know."

"No," says Sam, "I *don't.* I think I do sometimes, I think I know everything, but then I turn around and wonder if I'm at all in touch since you went with the Bigelows. I want to know, Ollie. And I don't." Then in a smaller voice, he asks, *"Do I?"*

"Aw, come on, you know you *know,* Sam," says Ollie, smiling at him. "Nobody but you *does.* It's you and me, right? You're the one who takes care of me, really. I know it. The Bigelows do too. I mean, you can tell them what to do and everything."

"Yeah. I can tell them what to do." Sam watches Ollie, and sighs. "Well, that's something, I guess."

"Sure it is," says Ollie. He makes himself wait a few seconds. "Will you tell them to let me go out?"

"Tell me why it's important."

Ollie frowns. "What do you mean?" He adds: "That's the kind of question *they'd* ask."

"It's the kind of question people responsible for you would ask," Sam says. "People who wanted to make you happy because they understood you, not just because they could see what you wanted."

Ollie sits for a moment, thinking. "It's not that important," he says. "I guess it doesn't matter much after all." He starts to get up.

Sam reaches out and restrains him. Ollie looks straight ahead. "Ollie," Sam says.

"What?"

Sam thinks. "This is the first time you've ever told me something you want. I've just realized that. It's the first time you've ever *asked* me for anything. Or the Bigelows either, I bet."

"I didn't say anything to them," Ollie puts in.

"All the more reason." Sam nods. "All the more reason I should be listening, isn't it? You're the guy who just accepts it all, aren't you? You go along, and ask for nothing. You . . . it must be faith," says Sam. Ollie looks up sharply. Sam isn't watching him; he's gesturing with his hands. As he goes on to explain, Ollie looks quickly down again. "It's faith that you will be taken care of. Trust. Trust in others."

He is looking at Ollie now with something like

awe. "Nothing," says Sam. "You've asked me for nothing before. How could I miss that?"

"It doesn't matter," says Ollie. "Nobody's, like, keeping score."

Sam shakes his head. "I *should* be," he says. "If for no other reason than to appreciate your faith."

Neither boy speaks for a while. Then, just as Sam is drawing breath to say something, Ollie says, "I don't know why I need to do what I do, Sam." He looks over at his brother. His face is twisted simply into a terrible frown, and his eyes look lost. "It's like—I can either *do* stuff, or I can worry about 'why.' I don't *like* 'why.' I don't *like* it. Do I have to? Do I have to *know*?" Slow tears squeeze from his eyes and stop on his cheeks as if unwilling to go far. Sam, with a wordless cry, takes Ollie roughly into his arms. Ollie keeps saying, "Do I have to know? Do I have to know?"

Sam, holding him close, finally says, "No. No no no no. You don't. Knowing—it's my job, Ol. You're free; maybe it's the best thing I can give you." He pulls back from Ollie. "Leave it to Sam. I'll talk to the Bigelows. I'll tell them to let you do what you want."

"Thanks," says Ollie, after a moment. After another, they separate.

As Ollie buttons his jacket, Sam smiles and says, "Hey, Ol?"

"Yeah?"

"You . . . you knew you could count on me, right?"

"Sure," says Ollie, looking at him. "Sure, Sam."

"That's something, isn't it?"

Ollie blinks. "You bet," he says. "Sure. Hey, Sam—see you later."

WEDNESDAY

N I N E

The skinny man with the skewed eyes stops in the middle of a sentence and darts to a corner of the cluttered room. He reaches behind six blue paper boxes and a pile of iron galleys and comes up with a black telephone receiver. Grinning past the cigarette in his teeth at the half dozen men—and one boy—in the room, he says grandly, "Columbia Printery, how the hell are you and what can I do to help?"

The men laugh. "Can't nobody *hear* that antique phone in this place except Pepper," says one, hunkering over his coffee at a counter covered with inky type forms tied with string.

"Can't nobody hear *any*thing over those presses," says another.

"I don't know," says a third. "Way I feel today, I reckon I'd jump if somebody slipped a greased cork out of a bottle of Ace-Hi in the way-back room ve-ry slowly."

Everyone laughs, except the boy. He simply smiles. It is Sam.

The man cal'ed Pepper has laid down the telephone and walked over to a crowded coat hook near the door. "Whoa, Pepper," says one heavy fellow. "Where you heading?"

Pepper jumps into a battered suede jacket with a quick couple of motions. "Man named Ralph at the Ramada just ordered a drink and he doesn't want to drink it," he says. "Watching it sit on the bar from where he's standing at the pay phone. Told him to hold on to the phone until I got there. Any of you want to sing him a Steemer-ass hymn while I'm on the way, pick up that receiver. He'll be glad of the company." He nods at the boy. "Sam, you take over that lawyer's stationery on the Chandler & Price; he's coming in twenty damn minutes. Cut off the Heidelberg and I'll finish those tickets when I get back."

The heavy man has slid from his stool and taken

a large wool coat down from the hook. "I'll go, Pepper," he says. "You stay with your tickets." He huffs as he pulls the coat on. "As you can see, I need the work."

"You need the *drink*," somebody says, and they laugh, including the heavy man.

Pepper says, "Hell, Wally, I already got my coat on."

" 'Yeah, Wally, I wasted six tenths of a second putting it on and now I gotta waste six tenths taking it off for no damn reason,' " squeals a tall black man in Pepper's quick speech. More laughter.

But Pepper is already out of the coat and through the low door leading to the back room. His voice snaps back at them: "I'll make some coffee in case that indecisive motel-loving son-of-a-biscuit drunk wants to come back for a cup. Bring him if he needs the company."

"Righto, Pepper," says Wally, opening the door. "Later, gents." He steps out to a smattering of fare-wells.

Sam follows Pepper into the back room. "Mr. Culpepper," he says, "should I go back to the tickets or take over the stationery as you said?"

"Better spell me on the stationery," Pepper says without looking up. "We need speed now, not beauty."

Sam walks over to the press, a large iron contraption of spinning wheels and clanking plates, which has been rolling at medium speed during all of the talk in front, as has the even larger press to its right—though both have been disengaged from the printing stroke. Sam slips a piece of sandpaper onto the middle finger of his right hand and secures it with a rubber band; then with his left he pushes a large lever, and begins whipping paper in and out of the press in a careful rhythm. Right hand snaps blank page in; clank of printing stroke as type hits paper; left hand snatches printed paper out as right hand puts another piece in—and so on. After two minutes he glances at the clock on the wall above the press and at the counter clicking with each impression. With a quick jab of his left hand he pushes a thin handle as far as it goes. The press immediately jumps to a higher speed.

Culpepper slips the larger press back into gear. Its insertion and removal of paper is automatic, done by brass-decorated armatures that grip individual pieces of card stock with pneumatic suction. Near the two presses, the noise is loud and rhythmic.

"Well," Culpepper says, standing up from a check on the Heidelberg's lower paper holder, "how the hell is your mom?"

Sam gives a tiny start that throws off his inserting

hand, but he manages to straighten the page an instant before the type clunks into it. "She's fine," he says.

Culpepper lights a cigarette and leaves it in his mouth. "Damn well ought to be, considering what Soberlife charges," he says. "Ought to be suntanned too, and be able to play the piano and conjugate German verbs."

"She's sober," says Sam. "That's enough for now. I didn't have to pay much, anyway. The government took care of most of it."

"You're lucky your sorry father took off a while back, or you'd be paying for the rest of your life. Lucky you got that kid brother, too. As it is, I bet you just *did* qualify for the assistance." Culpepper processes a lungful of smoke with a quick inhale-exhale. "How is the kid? Like seeing his mom again?"

Sam pretends to concentrate on a tricky page placement. Culpepper watches the Heidelberg. Sam says, "He's fine."

"Everybody's so damn fine in alcoholic families I wonder why I stopped drinking," Culpepper says. "I thought I was giving my kids a break, but from what you say they probably didn't even notice. She's fine, he's fine, you're fine. You going to let the boy go foster? Time must be up soon."

Sam flicks him a glance. Culpepper just watches his press print tickets. Sam says, "It's up very soon."

Culpepper looks at him, then bends down and gives a gear a finger wipe during a half-second pause in its rotation. He stands back up, looking at the oil on his finger. "Sounds like I've put my finger on it." He grins and shows Sam the smudge.

Sam laughs, then takes a deep breath. "I don't know, Mr. C.," he says. "You put your finger *right* on it. I don't know."

They print for a while without talking. Culpepper seems completely occupied with his automatic press. Sam, at his manual one, seems to have too much spare time on his hands: He fidgets, grunts, sighs, and looks around a lot, all the while slipping paper in and slipping it out. Finally he says, "They haven't seen each other yet."

"She's only been out one day," says Culpepper, looking over the rims of his glasses at a ticket snatched from the pile stacked by the pneumatic arm. "What's the big-ass hurry?"

Sam frowns. "Well, I—" He looks at the man, then back at his press. "Actually I didn't plan to let them meet right away. I planned on *fighting* to keep them apart for a few days. Until I could, you know, structure things exactly *right.* For their reunion. Not to fight with Ollie, actually, because . . . I didn't tell him I was getting his mother out." He glances expectantly at Culpepper, who squints at the Heidelberg's counter and increases its speed a notch.

Sam goes on. "I thought I *would* have to fight with my mother, though. I thought she'd want to tear right over to wherever Ollie was and"— he shakes his head—"*see* him. *Hug* him. I don't know. I was going to resist. I had the plans. But I *junked* my plans. I offered to take her. It would have blown everything, but I offered."

Culpepper removes a stack of printed tickets. The pneumatic arm immediately begins another in the same spot. "She didn't want to go," he says.

"Right!" says Sam, incredulous. "Can you— She didn't want to. 'I'll catch Ollie later,' she said. 'Let's go get something to eat.'" Sam frowns, shakes his head. In a lower voice, as if to himself, he adds: "Cold, almost."

Culpepper, arms crossed, cigarette in his teeth slanting upward, turns his head and looks at Sam. One eye aims at the boy's face; the other aims at the middle of the room. Sam slips a look at them both, and keeps printing.

"Sounds to me, then," Culpepper says, "like you're back on the plan. Back in control."

Sam thinks for a moment. "Right," he says. He nods. "Yes."

Culpepper studies him for another moment, then turns his head back to his press.

A bell rings up front; the door has opened. Over the rattle of the presses a few voice notes penetrate the back room. The tones are good-humored, courteous.

"Wally brought him back," says Sam as he prints his last piece of stationery.

"Damn!" says Culpepper, glancing at the door. "I didn't make the fresh-ass coffee."

"I'll make it," says Sam, pulling the clutch lever and flipping the power switch. His press slows down and stops. The halving of the noise makes the shop seem quiet. A couple of laughs and a new voice cut through from the front.

"Make it strong," Culpepper says, removing another stack of tickets from the Heidelberg. "We don't know how close he came. Or even if he called on the first drink."

Sam measures coffee and water and turns on the coffee maker. It is very old. There is a new, more modern coffee maker sitting nearby, with a red bow stuck to the glass pot. It is covered with a thin layer of dust. A card hangs from the bow, with some printing on it in large type. The lines are off-center, slanted, and smeared; they read:

When the coffee is ready, Sam takes the pot and a clean cup and goes into the front room. The same men are sitting at the type-cluttered counter, hunkered over empty coffee cups. A new man, still wearing a neat tan overcoat over a white shirt and red tie, sits in the middle, looking happily around him and nodding at a story the tall black man is telling. Sam puts the cup in front of the new man and fills it with coffee. The man glances at him and says, "Thanks," with a gentle Southern accent—then stares. Sam smiles, and goes over to lean against a desk, watching the men.

After the story is over and the coffeepot has been passed, the new man says, "So—I guess what I don't understand is—where am I?" He laughs and the men laugh with him.

"The Washington, D.C., floating chapter of Alcoholics Anonymous's perpetual brunch," says one.

"Or, the Columbia Printery's boxing, folding, and stapling crew's perpetual coffee break," says another. More laughter.

The man smiles. "But—"

Wally says, "Let's go over it step by step. You called the number in the phone book under A.A."

"And you got a printshop."

"Which sent an overweight, sluggish drunk to pick you up, and he, without benefit of stimulating conversation, brought you—"

"—here. Where you find a circle of fine fellows of great cheer, all apparently employed to sit on stools and drink joe."

"That sums it up pretty well," says the man. He looks around. "And you all are . . . ?"

"Alcoholics? Yes."

"*Sober* alcoholics," adds one.

"For now," says the tall man.

The man nods. "And—did any of you ever . . . you know, call like I just did . . . ?"

"Almost all of us," says Wally. He leans closer to the new man. "And—*we never left!*" The others laugh. The new man joins in, uncertainly.

"The truth is," says the black man, "there's sort of a rotating bunch of us. On any given day at any given time you'll find, oh, two to seven of us in here for an hour or two." He looks around. The men nod. "We hang out. Shoot the breeze. Drink some coffee." He winks.

"Stay out of the taverns," says the new man. The

black man smiles, and inclines his head. The new man says, "And do you *work* here?"

A loud laugh cuts through from the back room. Wally says, "We just kind of raise the tone of the place."

"And we do a little junk work. The owner's a drunk too, so he knows better than to expect too much." Laughter.

The new man looks around in wonder, and shakes his head. "It's great," he says.

"Glad you like it," the black man says. "Be here at seven thirty tomorrow morning. You got two cups of coffee to pay for now, with hard labor."

The man laughs. "Tomorrow morning I'll be selling industrial carpet at a hospital in Baltimore," he says. "Sober, too." He glances around again. His eyes snag on Sam. He leans closer to Wally. "One thing," he says.

"Sure," says Wally. "Only don't whisper. We got no secrets."

"Well," says the man, "that's the thing." He looks at a couple of the faces, at Sam, and back at Wally. "I mean, you guys talk pretty frankly. But, you know, what about"—he nods toward Sam—"the boy?"

There is a moment of silence. The tall black man,

looking at the new fellow, reaches a long arm back and hooks Sam, pulling him into the circle. The man next to him throws an arm around Sam's shoulders too.

Sam looks at the countertop. The black man, still looking at the salesman, says, "*What* boy?"

The man next to him smiles at the new man and says, "Do *you* see a boy?"

The new man stares at Sam. Sam continues to study the countertop. Finally he raises his eyes and meets the man's stare.

"No," says the man.

"That's right. Ain't nobody here," says the black man, giving Sam a slow waggle, "but us old men."

T   E   N

The wooden door with the frosted glass opens and swings inward. Ollie stands on the other side. His hands are in his pockets; it's as if the door swung open by itself, though it is an old door with a knob that must be turned. Ollie shows no sign of having opened it, but he also shows none of the swagger that should accompany such a pretense. The counselor in the office frowns. Ollie just stands there, blinking behind his spectacles.

"Come in then, Oliver," says the counselor. She frowns until Ollie has closed the door and sat down across the desk from her. Then her expression relaxes into a clinical neutrality.

She looks at a paper on her desk. "You hit Suzanne Warner."

Ollie nods.

"Well, we're going to talk about it."

"Okay," says Ollie.

The counselor nods. She moves the paper on her desk an inch to the left, purses her lips, then says, "Did she tease you about anything personal—maybe something painful?"

"No," says Ollie.

"Did she call you—or, say, a member of your family—any names?"

Ollie shakes his head.

The woman looks into an open file beside the paper on her desk. "Do you have any nicknames? Do the children call you anything, sometimes?"

Ollie thinks. "Sometimes they call me Owl," he says. "Sometimes Owlie." He points to his face. "The glasses."

"Yes," says the counselor. "I see. And when they call you Owl, or Owlie, does this bother you?"

"No," says Ollie.

"It doesn't? Do you *like* being called the name of a kind of bird?"

Ollie shrugs. "Birds are okay."

The woman thinks. "Do you ever *feel* like bird?" she asks intently.

"No."

"Do you ever wish you could fly? To get away? To soar above everything here in this life?" She watches him keenly.

"No," says Ollie politely.

The counselor watches him for a few moments, then nods. She looks at her file, then without looking up says, "Tell me about Suzanne."

Ollie blinks. "What about her?"

"Anything. What comes to your mind when you hear her name?"

Ollie thinks. "Nothing. I mean, other than, you know, Suzanne."

"What is she to you?"

Ollie shrugs. "She's a person in my class. She's okay."

The counselor looks up sharply with a frown. "A 'person'? Isn't she a *girl*?"

Ollie wrinkles his forehead. "Well," he says, "sure."

"Did you hit her because she's a girl? Did you feel something that made you want to strike out against a female?"

"No."

"Are you certain? Isn't there some . . . resentment

that comes out when you have the opportunity to strike a female?"

"No," says Ollie. Then he politely adds, "I don't resent you, either."

The counselor stares for a second, then flashes a quick, nervous smile. "No. Good. Of course not. Thank you." She looks down at her file, glances back up at Ollie, then resumes the study of the file.

After a moment, she looks at him again. "Oliver. Do you feel that hitting someone—which is a pretty *strong* thing to do, the way onions have a strong *flavor*—do you feel it is a way of taking control of him or her? You know—of being the boss?"

Ollie blinks. "No," he says. "I wouldn't want to be the boss."

"Are you certain? Being in charge—that doesn't sound good to you?"

"No," says Ollie. He shakes his head. "I don't think I'd like that at all."

The counselor sighs. She runs her eye over the paper on her desk. "No," she murmurs to herself, "no, no, and no." She looks up at the boy. "Are you mysterious, Ollie?"

"No."

"Of course not," the counselor says. "All right. You can go."

*　*　*

The counselor slips between two pairs of convers-
ing women, edges behind a man wearing a sweat-
shirt and a whistle on a lanyard as he reads the sports
page at a long table, and reaches the coffee machine.
She pours coffee into a white plastic cup, puts three
cubes of sugar into it, and takes a plastic spoon from
a box. She looks around quickly, then makes her way
back to a soft chair in one corner. Two more women
enter the lounge; they fall into conversation with one
of the pairs already talking. The counselor stirs her
coffee.

"So," says a voice above her, "how's the first week
gone?"

The counselor looks up. A red-cheeked blond
woman in a white uniform is standing near her chair,
smiling.

"Hi," says the counselor.

"My name's Gretchen," says the woman. "School
nurse. May I join you?"

"Yes," says the counselor, nodding toward the
chair next to her. "Please."

The woman sits down, crosses her legs, and begins
to massage one ankle. "You'll have to pardon me,"
she says. "A slight sprain from a week ago. I coach

volleyball and I should *never* try to demonstrate tricky saves."

The counselor watches her deftly touching the joint. "I wish you could do that to my brain," she says.

The nurse stops massaging her ankle and rotates it. "Hard week, I bet. Tough to adjust to a new school."

The counselor groans. "Tough to adjust—" She hesitates, looks at the nurse. "I just wish I knew what they want me to *do!*"

The nurse uncrosses her legs and leans back. She looks at the counselor. "What do you mean? Is our system that different from your previous school's?"

"No," says the counselor, "not much, but what I'm talking about is . . . well, my training. My training versus the children's training, I suppose I could say."

"Ah," says the nurse. "You must be trained in counseling doctrinaire AOs."

"Yes," says the counselor fervently. "Exactly. And this is a school without"—she ticks them off on her fingers—"the Alcoholic Offspring Late Childhood Education Program, the Alcoholic Offspring Doctrine Code, the Alcoholic Offspring Cross-Subject Reference Matrix . . ." She spreads her hands in a gesture of helplessness, and lets them fall. "This place doesn't even have the ditsy little Soberlife Schooldays alternative. Why did they hire me?"

"Surely you knew this was a non-AO school. You must have talked about that during your interview."

The woman groans again. "I had checked the directory, but they asked so much about my AO experience that I didn't bother. I assumed it was one of those private schools that does AO unlisted. I mean—we discussed AO sans-parent counseling for forty-five minutes! At a fairly sophisticated level, too; the administrators here know as much as any administrators ever do, which, I grant you, usually isn't much. And there was more. One assistant principal asked at least ten questions about the Reference Matrix—"

"That was Joanne. She works half time in the Media Catalogue Center. She was probably scared to bits about overtime."

"Well, I can tell you, after the workout they gave me, I *had* to assume this was unlisted AO. It would have made me look as if I hadn't been paying *attention* if I asked." She takes a gulp of coffee, and shakes her head incredulously. "Then I arrive, and they set me up, and almost as an afterthought the headmaster tells me I will be practicing standard non-AO behavioral analysis. 'But'—you won't believe this—'but,' he says, 'with certain appropriate children, we hope you will add some *spice* to the practice with your expertise—if you know what I mean.'" The woman throws her hands up again. "As if kids were soup and the AO program was marjoram."

The nurse has been following this raptly. Now she gives the counselor a pat on the knee and says, "I think I understand."

The counselor looks at her. "Then tell me," she says seriously.

The nurse nods, and looks around the room. She smiles and waves at one woman near the coffee machine, and at the man, who says, "Hi, coach" to her. When they have turned back to what they were doing, she turns back to the counselor and says, "You are here, I'm afraid, to singlehandedly bootleg us into AO." She shakes her head and smiles wryly. "There's been something on the wire about this for a couple of years, but we didn't know it was coming up this fast. We thought they'd sort of phase out the tradition of accepting mostly students from sober homes and start bringing in more alcoholics' kids. There are only a few token ones now. Then, when the student body had changed enough, they'd announce they simply had to switch to AO to meet the needs of the students and parents and la dee da." She laughs, and pats the counselor's leg again. "They got you—and you should take this well—because they thought they could have it both ways for a while.

You must be a superb generalist counselor, in addition to your AO training."

The counselor shakes her head once. She looks grim. "But I'm not," she says.

"You're being modest."

"I'm being accurate." She puts her hand around the nurse's wrist and pulls her close. "I have *no* certification outside AO programs. My thesis was on the doctrinal interface between quantified behavior-analysis patterns and AOCLEP. Quantified! I am trained to deal with kids who are tested every week for theoretical knowledge of specific AO doctrine *and* behavioral adjustment in AO alignments. At my previous school, a kid would come in and say 'I aggressed on the math teacher's car in a third-level post-denial anger/pity syndrome, and I broke the windshield.' I would say 'What's your denial factor?' and he would say 'Eight,' and I would say 'Index of control achievement?' and he would say 'Six,' and I would know *exactly* what to do with him. And I mean *with* him: The AO is trained essentially as a co-counselor; he is at least a co-analyst. Now, what am I supposed to do with a kid who knows nothing except that he threw a rock at a car?"

The counselor is still squeezing the nurse's wrist. She looks down, sees her grasp on the other woman, and lets go. She sits back, and puts her hands up to the lower part of her face.

"It's a ridiculous position they've put you in," the nurse says quietly. "Especially as only about six percent of our kids are from alcoholic families."

"Actually," the counselor says, pulling her hands down, "those are the hardest ones."

"Because you recognize things you know how to treat within the doctrine?"

"Exactly. But I cannot use doctrine. I can only fumble along, trying to put the category-indexing questions into plain-sounding words. Which *nobody* gets. One kid today aggressed on a girl. He has a female parent in a sobriety institution, put there almost two years ago when this child was eight. He is in a foster home that looks suspiciously clean—probably what we call a high-denial sheen in the household. So when a kid like this hits a girl, there are three very clear possibilities—I won't go into them, but they key on a sexed association between parent and aggression object, crossed with factors of control quest and denial. And after two minutes I can tell this is a *very* evasive child. He is unbelievably cool; by far the greatest adjustment gift—that's a technical term you can figure out—that I have seen in years. He almost has me believing he is as innocent as he seems, but this fact that he has hit a girl for no reason—"

"Wait a minute," says the nurse. "Do you remember his name?"

"Well," says the counselor hesitantly, "the practice is supposed to be confidential—"

"That's AO practice," says the nurse quickly. "This, as you are so cruelly learning, is not AO practice. Here, I'll ask you—was his name Oliver?"

The counselor stares for a moment, then nods.

"He hit a girl? Was it Suzanne Warner?"

The counselor nods. The nurse nods too, and thinks for a moment. She looks at the counselor.

"He gave you no explanation?"

"No. I asked him a clear battery of—"

"Did you ever ask him 'Why did you hit Suzanne?'"

The counselor, looking confused, says, "No. Not like that. We are trained to avoid the frontal inquiry because it invites an astounding variety of denial devices—"

"Yes, yes, I'm sure." The nurse smiles. "Ollie said 'No' to all of your questions?"

"Yes."

The nurse laughs hard, and puts her arm around the counselor's shoulders. Then she looks across the room for a moment; when she spots a young woman with curly red hair, she waves. "Gail. Can you come here for a second?" The woman walks over to them, and questions the nurse with her green eyes.

The nurse says, "This is Gail, Ollie's teacher. This is Maria, the new counselor. We're talking about Ollie. Did you send him to her?"

"Yes," says Gail, "reluctantly. Ollie has never done a thing before now. The perfect kid if ever I saw one; absolutely disappears in school except to answer just enough questions to stay on the books. But he hit Suzanne Warner. Knocked her over a desk, knickers up. If it had been Donnie Allen I wouldn't have bothered you—he punches someone every other day, and I send him home—but the fact that Ollie is so harmless made the offense alarming."

"I see," says the counselor politely. Then she looks at the nurse.

The nurse asks Gail, "And Ollie said nothing to you about what Suzanne had done to provoke him?"

The teacher wrinkles her forehead and thinks. "No."

"Did you ask him for an explanation?"

"Well, I— No, not actually. I assumed the counselor would take care of that."

The nurse nods, and looks at both of them. "Well, it's a shame neither of you risked what you call 'the frontal inquiry.' Because if you had, Ollie would have said something like 'I hit Suzanne because I lost my temper after she stabbed me, once in each hand, with the point of a steel compass.'"

"What?" says Gail sharply. The counselor gapes.

The nurse nods. "This morning I treated Ollie for two punctures, one in each hand. They hadn't bled much, but I could see from some stains that he had been hiding his hands in his pockets. Probably while he was with you, Maria. I made him tell me how he got them by threatening to send him home and to the hospital."

The counselor thinks. "Yes," she says, "I never saw his hands."

"Maybe we should ask you why he wouldn't mention it," says the nurse.

The counselor is thinking. After a moment she says, "I said before that he was the coolest kid I've seen for years. There is a thing called the adjustment gift—the inclination to go along with whatever happens, never to stick out, to answer only the questions one is asked, to fit in at all costs. . . . He's a classic, it seems."

Gail is frowning. The nurse looks at each of them, and says, "And are such kids . . . troubled?"

"Deeply," says the counselor. "They require an immensely elegant treatment program—"

"Then we're not talking about Ollie," snaps Gail. They both look at her. She is glaring. "We are not talking about this kid—or *any* kid, for that matter, with all that AO junk. 'Elegant treatment,' indeed."

"Elegant is simply a term denoting a certain complexity and—"

"Yes, I can imagine," says Gail. She laughs coldly. "And 'good' is simply a term denoting a certain wholesome, stable, humble strength. It's not a flashy word; I'm sorry. It doesn't sound too scientific and it doesn't reflect nearly as well on the person who uses it, either. But it works here. Ollie is a good kid—the best."

She looks at each woman long and hard. "To screw up a simple good kid—especially one who had to keep his strength through the challenges Ollie has had—to screw him up with a lot of weird theory and doctrine would be *diseased.*" She points at the counselor. "And I'll see you out of this school if you pull that AO stuff on my kids. This is not an AO school yet."

She turns and goes. Within a minute, the other teachers in the lounge—all of whom have heard her outcry—follow, giving the counselor and the nurse hard looks.

They sit alone. The nurse glances at the other woman. "Well?" she says.

The counselor is looking after the teachers. "Well," she says. Then, in a moment, she adds: "This not an AO school yet. Unfortunately for Ollie, that does not mean he is not an AO."

"But he's unlisted," says the nurse.

"Right," says the counselor. "And he'll stay that way for now."

"Either that, or he'll stay simply *good.*"

The counselor thinks for another moment. "Sure," she says. "We'll see. And soon, I bet."

E L E V E N

Sam's mother enters the apartment, leaving the door open behind her, and walks straight to one of the chairs along the back wall. She drops into it, heavily, and sits with her arms on the chair arms, head back, eyes closed.

Sam walks in. He looks at her, then glances quickly around the apartment. He gives a start. Painted on the front wall is an open window looking out on a desert, represented by a flat expanse of tan sand with a single tall cactus in the middle.

He looks back at his mother, who has not moved

or opened her eyes; just as he's about to sputter an exclamation, she says, in an old-movie wise-guy voice, " 'It's a jungle out there, Mom.' " Then she opens her eyes and sits forward, smiling.

He's searching for words. All he comes up with is "I'll lose my deposit."

"You may not. If I live here forever, no one will ever check. But, come to think of it, then you won't get your deposit back anyway. So—let this be a lesson: Never front money for a drunk."

He looks at the wall again. "Is it oil?"

"Oh, for God's sake," she says. "No. It's cheap watercolor and will wash off. Give me some credit. I wouldn't *destroy* anything."

He looks at her, thinks for a moment, then takes off his coat and sits.

"I lied, didn't I?" she says, holding a hand to her mouth.

He shrugs.

She sighs, balls her hands into fists, and lightly taps the chair arms. "*Arrrr!*" she growls. "I can't get used to the fact that you can't trust me. It's hard to be so damn sober and keep in mind that it wasn't always so, and that everyone around me is thinking *Any minute she may go nuts! Is this it? Is that painting the first sign of her collapse? Back to chokey with her!* I mean, can I call myself 'responsible' if I trust myself? Or is acting like a humble insect the only way I can demonstrate my mature grasp of things?"

"No one is thinking all that about you," says Sam.

She reaches out for his hand and holds it. "You're sweet to say it, and I know you try, and you nearly make it, so that's close enough. I mean, at least you keep the doubt out of your eyes. But those women at the shop—they're all watching me as if I were suddenly going to snarl, sprout fangs, and sink them into the neck of my customers."

"Maybe I made a mistake, getting you that job."

She shakes his hand. "No, no, you were wonderful to do it. Don't let my bitching cause you any doubt about what you've done. You aren't responsible for those poor ladies, who evidently never heard of an alcoholic before."

"They haven't," he says.

"Did you tell them not to let me touch money?"

Sam flushes. "No! Why would I—"

"Okay, I believe you. They came up with the idea all on their own, I guess. At least six times today one of the salesladies dropped what she was doing and rushed over to snatch the money my customer was about to hand me for a routine sale. Two times the lady had to wedge herself between me and the customer. One of them even grabbed my hand just as it was about to catch a ten-dollar bill."

Sam smiles slightly. "Well, you can hardly blame them. Obviously you were going to take the cash and run madly into the street, waving it and screaming for booze." He pats her hand. "You know, I think they did you a favor, Mother."

"They did *you* a bigger one. I . . . I . . . I just don't know *where* I would have stopped!" She puts the back of a hand to her forehead and leans backward.

Sam, chin in hand, wrinkles his forehead studiously. "Probably when you reached a guilt-release viability index of 4," he says, "cross-referred with a repressed denial-negation acuity. Either then," he says, "or when your blood alcohol hit 1.5 and you passed out."

She is laughing. "Oh, but help! Help! I can feel an interdoctrinal gap growing in my pre-positivity recognition factors: I can't decide whether to call myself 'sober' or 'acutely postalcohol,' so I can't calculate the related indices of integrated stability. And it's nearly time for my six o'clock self-analysis battery! What's a poor girl to do?"

"Take a drink," says Sam, "and wing it."

She hoots. He smiles and watches her laugh. When she finishes, she sighs. "Ah. Thank God you're still fun."

"Still?" says Sam seriously. "You mean, I was fun in the past? *Fun?*"

She looks at him for a long moment. "Fun," she says. "Always. Well—except for when you found God the year before your father left, and walked around behind me quoting Matthew and Luke when I burned the biscuits or dropped a teacup and let fly a 'darn' or a 'drat.' "

"Did I do that?"

"Damn right. For probably two months. What a pain."

"But—I must have been only eight or so—"

"Old enough for sanctimony. Which, of course, you come by naturally."

"I remember something about church and stuff, but quoting the Bible . . ."

"Just the New Testament," his mother says, holding up a finger. "And not, I suspected, always accurately. You would make up stuff when your memory slipped, very scriptural-sounding passages, full of 'verily' and 'it came to pass.' And long quotations from Christ himself. You had the spirit, you had the lingo, and you didn't hesitate to fill in the blanks. I rather enjoyed those parts."

"Jesus!" Sam exclaims.

"The very man."

"No," he says, rubbing his forehead, "I mean . . ." He laughs. So does she. He asks, "Why did I stop? Because Dad left?"

"Oh, no," she says. "You dropped it well before he joined the missionaries. In fact, that was the reason he left—he was so disappointed in your failure to share the Lord with him, he went off to the Eskimos to seek a *true* son in the Spirit."

Sam sits up, eyes wide. His face is white. "He . . . That was why he . . . It was me?"

His mother sighs contentedly. "No, actually. That wasn't it at all. I was just running a quick check on your associative-guilt matrix. Doing just fine, I see." She grins at him. He groans, but looks at least partly relieved. After a moment she says, "The real reason you quit was Ollie."

Sam sits up. "Ollie? You mean"—he is excited—"you mean, I loved him so much I didn't need Jesus anymore, or something like that?"

She laughs. "Not exactly. You tried it for a while—tried making him the object of your perfect grace. But soon you discovered it was much more fun to tease him than to adore him. And of course teasing doesn't mesh with being Little Jesus. . . ."

"Tease? I never *teased* him!"

"Well," she says judiciously, "perhaps 'torment' *would* be a better word."

"No." Sam is adamant. "I never did."

"Poo. You tore his tiny well-being to bits. Constantly. You were *brilliant* at it."

"But . . ." He glares at her. "Why didn't you stop me?"

She shrugs. "I thought it would be good for him. He always was too damned *solid*. He just sat there, broadcasting humorless equanimity. He was begging for it."

Sam gapes. "You let me—his big brother, who should be watching out for him—*tease* this tiny baby?"

"Right." She nods firmly. "Put toys just out of reach, peel bananas in front of him and give him the skins first, all that sort of thing."

Sam thinks, agitated. "Was I, you know, giving him positive learning experiences?"

"Absolutely not. You were having a good laugh at his expense."

Sam is gesturing with his hands, searching for words. "But—I wasn't, you know, really *mean* or anything."

"Oh, yes you were. Mean as a snake in May." She looks at him, and pats his leg. "But don't worry. Most of the time we adored him together—*spoiled* him together. And the teasing *was* good for him."

"How?"

"Second children need to be abused by siblings. It's a tradition with grand precedent. Torture at the hands of an older brother makes a kid careful, cunning, and independent. I'm sure there are studies, *lots* of them."

Sam thinks for a minute. "But why, in this case, did the parent *assist* the sibling?"

She shrugs. "Maybe I'd had a drink or two and got into the spirit of the game."

He shakes his head. "That's wrong. You never drank around Ollie."

She stares at him. "How do *you* know that?"

He smiles slightly. "It's true. It's true, isn't it?"

She leans back and closes her eyes. After a few moments she says, "Yes."

"I worked it out recently. It was one of those things, those patterns, that you don't recognize right away. One of those things that kind of haunt you on the edge of your thought. So one day I sat down and made a list of the times you were drunk. In my head, not on paper, but I got them all. And I went back through and remembered that for every one of them, Ollie was either securely bedded down or gone. He was at my father's parents' house, or he was at that Japanese music camp, or he was out to dinner with the mom of one of his nursery school friends. Remember the two nights he was in the hospital for his tonsils? I do."

"How?" she says. "How can you remember me drinking on a particular night when Ollie was out eating pizza with Freddy Wade and his parents? Or a couple hundred other times?"

He shrugs. "I remember. You don't forget things like that." She winces. He continues. "Anyway—all these times, I thought the same thing: *Thank goodness Ollie isn't here for this.* Every time I thought this! And it never clicked that it was . . . a series. It never came through. Each time I thought it was a strange coincidence, Ollie gone and you drunk." He pauses. Then he says, "Dad was gone too. I realized this, and at first I thought it was because he saw you start, and left—or at least that he knew it was coming, and got out of the way." He looks at her. "Now I don't think that anymore." He swallows. "I think you waited."

"Clear them all out," she says. "Leave room for the buzz."

"No," says Sam. "Not all."

"No," she says, looking at him. "Not Sambo." They watch each other for a moment. She says, "When did you have this revelation?"

"About a month ago."

She raises her eyebrows. "And you decided to get me *out*? You realized I only got drunk in front of you, and you sprang me from the safe confines of permanently subsidized 'treatment'?" She shakes her head. "Jeez, kid—you've got a pretty warped sense of revenge."

Sam looks at the front wall for a while. He says, "It wasn't that you only got drunk around me. That isn't what the revelation was."

"No? What was it? That I always wore shoes with rubber soles and parted my hair on the left? That I always struck matches toward me rather than away when lighting cigarettes while my content was above 1.5? What?"

Sam says, "That you were in control."

She stares. "That I was in *control*?"

He nods, but he does not meet her eyes. "That you could *time* it. That . . . that your drinking wasn't like a hurricane or a tree falling or something that just happened in a flash out of nowhere. That it was something you—*did.*" He looks at her. His eyes hold tears. "*That* was the revelation. For a long time I thought of you as a victim. Now I had to see you as a perpetrator." He looks down. "It's hard enough, not thinking that to *begin* with. But I managed, you know? I managed to feel sorry for you. Not to blame you." He sighs.

She watches him. "And now you do. Blame me, I mean."

He shakes his head. "No. Not really. I couldn't go *that* far in reverse." He smiles briefly. "Four straight-A years of AO classes got *something* through to me. In very big ways, you are a victim—of the

119

disease, and all that. But—I guess I felt I could expect more from you now." He looks at her. "Before, I felt you couldn't control anything. You did a lousy job with the shopping, the money, the meetings with my teachers, the car pools for baseball practice, everything. It was okay. I understood that losing control of one thing—alcohol—meant everything else was blown too. And it was easy for me to, you know, help out. An eight-year-old can balance a checkbook. A nine-year-old can buy the groceries. A ten-year-old can talk with his teachers himself." He looks down. "I could control everything except the thing *you* couldn't control. The drinking."

"That's a lot in common," she says.

He glances sharply at her. "So I thought."

"Uh-oh."

"And now I suddenly realized that you *did* have some control, of the one thing I thought excused everything else." He laughs once, incredulously, raising his hands. "I mean, you let the easy stuff slide, and you had a secret handle on the hard thing. What was I, a sucker or something?"

"A victim," she says quietly. "Not a perpetrator."

He gives no sign of having heard her. "So, I decided to get you out." He looks at her, a struggle for sternness in every feature of his face. "I decided I could expect a few promises."

"Promises are easy."

"Not when you know what's at stake," he says. "It's the 'slammer' on one side, and Ollie on the other."

She looks at him. "Ollie. Just Ollie."

He nods. "Ollie and Soberlife. I hate to sound so hard about it. But it's time for Ollie to get on with his life. And he's in a good foster situation, and they want him, and the time to let them have him is now. If they are going to get him."

"Why shouldn't they?"

He gapes at her. Then he flushes, and points a shaking finger. "Don't mock them," he says.

"I'm not mocking anything," she says, flushing a bit herself. "I'm asking a sincere question."

"No mother of . . . of Ollie could possibly ask that question sincerely."

She studies him. "Of course not. Any mother would jump at the chance to promise anything for a shot at Ollie—just Ollie."

"You're damn right she would." He glares at her. She holds his stare thoughtfully.

After a minute she says, "So what's the deal? What's the promise? Sobriety forever?"

"I wish," he says. "But I know better."

She smiles to herself. "Thanks for that."

"The promise," he says, "is to keep up with what

you started. To continue the decision you made a long time ago. It was a wise decision. If you could stick to it then, you can stick to it now." He raises his eyebrows. "Do you know what I mean?"

"Let's see—to part my hair on the left?"

"To stay sober around Ollie." He lifts his hands slightly, palms up. "That's all. Never to drink when he is at all likely to see you. It won't be that hard. There are a lot of other times."

"When I'll be free to exercise my control and get drunk. Great," she says. "You even have my setbacks scheduled for me. You're a responsible son of a bitch, aren't you?"

"I am a realistic son of a bitch," he says.

She nods at him. "And you're going to make sure Ollie never becomes the same."

He thinks for a moment. "That's right," he says. "What's wrong with that?"

"Probably nothing," she says. "At least, for Ollie."

"Aw," he says, a bit sardonically, "I don't think you come out of it so poorly. As far as I can see, you get quite a bit—life outside the institution, a reason to stay sober most of the time, and Ollie."

"I wasn't thinking of me," she says. "But never mind. Let's go eat. I'm hungry after pushing elegance to fat women all day. And no Laotian food—

the staff at Soberlife is entirely from Laos, and I've had *matawir* enough for a lifetime."

She gets up—her coat is still on—and walks out, leaving the door open behind her. After a moment, he stands up, gets his coat from the closet, and walks to the door. He hesitates, and looks at the painting on the front wall. He walks over to it, and bends to look closely at the surface. He wets a finger, and rubs at a corner. He looks at the finger. It is stained. He nods, turns back toward the door, and leaves.

T W E L V E

Tonight Ollie is walking on a street that runs along the river. He walks on the landward side of the roadway, in the shadow of small warehouses of dark brick. The moon is full.

Ollie is carrying the case of a musical instrument. Despite the load, he walks silently on the uneven sidewalk, staying nimbly within the thin moon shadows of the warehouses. He crosses the ends of roads and alleys angling down into this street, but he never glances at them; he seems to know his way.

He walks for blocks. There is no sound, except an

occasional indistinct noise from a bus on a street far above this one, in a part of the city no less dark, but more populated.

But as he follows a curve to the right, he slows to a creeping walk. He stops.

From a few yards ahead, around the angle of the next building, comes a faint murmur. Voices. Two voices.

Ollie creeps through the shadows until he can see who is there. He stops.

Sitting on the wall, looking out over the river with their backs to him, are a young man and a young woman. The woman is speaking, and the man, sitting a few feet away, is nodding. Ollie cannot hear what she is saying; her tone has a forced lightness. She finishes. The young man nods a few more times, sneaks a quick glance at her, and stares out at the water. She stares too. There is silence.

A minute later, the young man begins to speak. He, too, sounds nervous. The young woman begins to nod. This continues for a few minutes. At one point, she laughs hesitantly. The young man finishes. She stops nodding. They stare at the water.

Ollie watches, still as the shadows that hide him. After several silent minutes, he sees the young man bend forward, and hears a clink. The man straightens up, and places on the stone wall between himself and the young woman a glass bottle full of pale liquid.

He bends forward again. The young woman watches him. He comes up with a stemmed glass in each hand. He places them beside the bottle, which he opens.

Now the young man pours some of the liquid into one of the glasses. This he then hands, with a smile, to the young woman. She takes it. The man pours liquid into the remaining glass, then puts the bottle down. Its neck catches moonlight and shines, as do the surfaces of the liquid in the glasses.

The man picks up his glass, and holds it toward the woman. She extends hers, until the glasses have lightly touched with a *tink*. Watching each other, the man and woman drink.

Ollie watches. The young man pours more. He says something. The young woman laughs—not stiffly, this time—and replies. The young man smiles, mutters something, and they both laugh. They drink again from their refilled glasses. A conversation begins. They talk, making gestures, looking fully at each other and the river, laughing from time to time. They finish the liquid in their glasses; he pours again.

Their talk comes spontaneously now. Ollie watches, his eyes wide open in the shadows. Once, when the two people laugh and lean their heads together, Ollie smiles; another time, when the young man makes a sweeping gesture, loses his balance, and nearly falls off the wall, Ollie involuntarily reaches out a hand. The young woman does so too, and grabs the man's arm to pull him back.

When the third glasses have been finished, the young man suddenly swings his legs back over the wall and jumps down into the street. He holds out a hand for the young woman to join him; with a giggle, she slides her legs across the top of the wall and slips down beside him. The young man makes a sweeping bow. The young woman smiles, inclines her head, and drops into a curtsy. Then he takes one of her hands, slips one arm around her waist, and begins to dance.

They dance. Ollie watches. They dance, in no pattern, but not without grace. Certainly they enjoy themselves: this Ollie can see by their flashing eyes in the moonlight, and the glint of their smiles. Ollie finds himself bobbing his head to a rhythm they seem to be seeking. They are not finding the rhythm together, though. Before he really knows he has done so, Ollie quietly opens the music case, removes the parts of a saxophone, and quickly assembles it.

Watching the dancers, he licks the reed of his instrument, and places the mouthpiece in his mouth.

He begins to play. The high, windy sound lifts into the air above the dancers, and Ollie immediately strikes a rhythm, the rhythm the dancers seem to be seeking with their slightly unsynchronized steps. The tune is lyrical but undirected; it wanders, but it holds to the rhythm.

The dancers do not even look in the direction of the music. Yet they notice it, for as they smile at each other, their steps begin to match. Ollie plays. He watches them as he makes the music. They look only at each other, spinning, bouncing, stepping from surprise to surprise in their movement. At one point the young man swings the woman in a sudden lurch toward the wall, and darts his arm out to grasp the bottle. He drinks from it and holds it for her to drink from, both of them laughing, spilling it as they move. They finish it; Ollie hears the bottle fall to the street and shatter. The dancers do not seem to notice.

They are closer together now. The young man has both arms around the young woman's shoulders; she has both arms around his waist. Their heads are touching.

Yet their rhythm has gotten worse. Ollie watches this, and plays more simply, less melodically, beat by beat. Still they seem unable to find the rhythm together. In fact, they lurch from time to time, or stumble: Ollie winces when this happens, and twice he clenches his mouth, producing a cutting *skreer* from his mouthpiece. He increases his loudness. The dancers do not respond. They keep moving merrily, but with less and less grace. They stumble, and the man goes down on one knee, nearly pulling the woman over. Ollie bites his reed. His saxophone bleats. But the dancers are back on their feet, bouncing again, laughing at their slip.

Ollie's reed is split. The notes he blows now begin to shriek. He watches the dancers. They refuse to match. He blows harder. He blows loud, simple notes. The melody is gone: Now he plays the crudest kind of cadence. The river seems to follow. The people do not. Ollie squeals through his mouthpiece. The dancers never look his way, never get in step. Yet they keep dancing, closer and closer in their embrace. They seem to take the shrieks for granted, as they took the initial melody. They do not even stop, or turn, or look up, when Ollie takes the saxophone from his mouth and the sound stops, and he stands, for a long time, watching them in silence.

THIRTEEN

Sam is walking with his hands in his pockets and his head down, past taverns, stores, cheap restaurants. He looks up slightly. Ahead of him is a familiar sight: a drunk, unable to keep his feet under him, being half carried, half pulled down the street. Sam moves to the side to slip by the two people on their left.

As he is passing them, eyes down again, fists jammed deep, he hears a voice call: "Hey! Hey, boy! God, what's your name . . ." He is past, and has swung back onto the sidewalk in front of them, when the man calls: "Sam! That's it. Sam! Hey!"

He slows but keeps walking, turning his head. Waving at him is the industrial carpet salesman who was in the printery this afternoon; his white shirt and red tie still look crisp beneath the tan raincoat. With a sudden cold flash, Sam looks at the drunk man, who is on his knees, one arm abandoned to the salesman's ineffective grasp. It is Archie, Mr. Culpepper's tall black friend. Sam sighs and stops.

"He said he's been sober six *years*," says the man, looking lost. "What can we do? Jesus. He said it's *six years*. He told me that in the printshop. We were all talking about how long it had been. He'd been the second longest of everybody. How . . ."

Sam walks over and takes Archie's other arm. Putting his weight beneath the elbow and using the upper arm as a stiff lever, he springs Archie upright. "Do this," he tells the salesman, who copies him. Archie is up, but he is not easy to move. He is large, and his body is limp. He coughs twice and brings up some mucus, which he spits sloppily onto his chest. Sam glances clinically at it.

"God help him" says the man. "I didn't think anybody could get this drunk." He makes a hollow groan.

Sam looks across Archie's chest at him. "Are you pretty new at this or something? I thought you were an alcoholic."

"Not like *this*," the man says with a grimace. He looks at Archie. Archie swings his vaguely alert eyes toward the man. The man looks away and says, "I thought if you stayed sober that long you never wanted it again."

Sam laughs as they propel Archie forward in heavy jerks. "Man, what kind of a dry-out program did *you* use? Something from a magazine ad?"

"I didn't use any *program*," the man says, in a hurt tone. "I just stopped drinking six months ago. Kind of by myself."

"Oh," Sam says. "Well . . . that's okay, then. I mean—you know, there's a whole . . . science, almost, about this, and I assumed you knew—"

"I don't know anything," the man says. "I just don't drink anymore. That's all. I have no idea what to do with . . . with this." He looks at Archie, who spits again.

"Well, I do," says Sam. "There's a sober bar over there. If we can get him decent in an hour, we'll take him home. If we can't, we'll check him into treatment at the admittance station around the corner. Come on, Archie." They jerk through several more steps.

"Can't we just call all his friends from the printshop?" says the man. "I mean—he's all alone; they're the ones who could understand and help—"

"You're a drunk; do *you* understand this?" says Sam. He gives Archie a shake.

"Well," the man stammers, "no—"

"Nobody understands this," says Sam, "least of all drunks. Watch the curb here."

They lift Archie's feet, one at a time, and shuffle him over toward a wide, doorless entry. Beyond is a well-lit room from which come whiffs of eucalyptus-scented disinfectant and coffee. "We were just *walking*," says the salesman, "joking and stuff, and he just wanted to buy some cigarettes and he didn't come back and I went in and—"

"Look out," says Sam.

Archie has suddenly found his legs; he spears them into the ground and jerks free. Eyes casting about, he balls up a fist and launches a wild, wheeling punch at the carpet salesman, who covers his head and yowls. Archie's large fist thunks him on the shoulder and caroms off, and Archie spins straight down. His head hits the sidewalk with the sound of dropped fruit.

"Damn it," says Sam, "get him up again. Don't let him pass out."

They jack him up with their arms. Sam looks at his face closely, and lifts one of his drooping eyelids.

"His nose is broken," says Sam, "but it's not bleeding much. He's still conscious—or at least he's not really passed out. Let's get him inside."

They jerk and slide Archie through the entryway. In the bright room deep benches run along the walls; on the floor in front of them runs a foot-wide rectangular trough with blue water running in it. It hisses. At one end of the room is a low fiberglass counter. Near it, on some stools, a few men sit quietly in white coats, smoking cigarettes, waiting for something. Behind the counter is a large stainless steel coffee machine. A man in a white undershirt leans forward on tattooed arms showing a lot of sinew. He, too, smokes.

There are no other drunks on the benches. Sam and the salesman lower Archie onto a bench. Sam hands the salesman some money, and sits quickly beside Archie, who is trying to lie down. "Get some coffee and four towels," he says. The man nods, looks at the money, looks at Sam, looks at Archie. Sam, peering again under Archie's eyelids, glances back. "Go on!" he says.

The salesman goes to the counter, asks for three coffees. The man behind the counter blinks at him a few times, shakes his head, shrugs, and fills three mugs from the machine. The mugs have covers on them and a wide, flat straw rising from the lid. The salesman asks for four towels. The man nods. He takes the money, slides some change and the coffee mugs across the counter. The salesman takes them and says, "What about the towels?" The sinewy man rolls his eyes, and nods toward Archie. The salesman turns. One of the white-coated men is putting a steaming tin bucket near Sam. The salesman mutters thanks and goes over to the boy.

"Here's the coffee," he says. Sam, who is pinching Archie's lower lip, looks up.

He shakes his head. "Why did you—" Laughter comes from behind them, at the counter. The salesman blushes. Sam lowers his voice and says, "Thanks." He takes a coffee, holds Archie by the chin with one hand, and tilts the mug in with the other. Archie swallows twice and twists away. Sam takes his hand away but grabs him loosely by the lapels, watching him.

The salesman has taken the lid off one of the two coffees. He is about to sip it when Sam says, without looking at him, "Don't drink it."

The salesman hesitates, frowns. "Why not?"

"Here's why not," Sam says. Archie gurgles, and Sam neatly pulls him forward by his coat, leaning him forward but keeping the drunk's arms pinned back. Archie is bug-eyed; his mouth gapes. Suddenly he vomits tremendously, a single stream of fluid.

Sam has held him so that it lands exactly in the trough. It disappears into the blue water without creating the slightest stain.

Sam waits a moment, and leans Archie back. He wipes the drunk's face with a hot towel and looks at a clock on the wall. Archie groans. Sam glances at him. "Wake up, Archie," he says. Archie groans.

Sam looks up at the salesman. "It contains an emetic," he says.

"A what?"

"Something to make you throw up," says Sam. He looks at the clock, picks up the coffee again, and tries to give Archie another dose. This time Archie flails at the mug, which falls out of Sam's hand onto the bench. Sam picks it up, still holding Archie with his other hand, but now by the hair. "Pull his teeth open," he says. He glances at the salesman. The man nods, sits down, and gingerly puts a hand on Archie's chin. Archie snarls and snaps at him like a wolf; Sam says, "Good," and swiftly gets the mug into the drunk's bite. He tilts it, pulling upward on Archie's hair. Two more swallows go down.

Seconds later, Archie vomits again. The boy holds him as before. He repeats the process a third time, tying Archie's hands with the fourth towel to keep him from rubbing his swollen nose.

"Damn it," Sam says, after a long look into Archie's face. "He's still going out. Do you have any idea how much he drank?"

The salesman, who cannot take his eyes off Archie's nose, says, "Maybe four doubles while I was there. Fast. I wasn't with him in that place but maybe ten minutes. He was in there ten before I went in. I kept hoping he'd come out any minute and I wouldn't have to go."

Sam nods. "Was it bug juice?"

"What?"

"Bug juice—a blend of unflavored grain alcohol with a synthetic-alcohol distillate, a little amphetamine, and a little synthetic morphine. It smells like cockroach spray. The alcohol gets you drunk, the speed keeps you running, the dope smooths you out—and you almost but never quite die every time you drink it." He looks up at the salesman with a grim smile. "Not your drink, eh?"

"I drank rum," the man says. He hesitates, then he asks: "How do you *know* all this?"

Sam studies Archie. "My mother is a drunk," he says, without looking up.

"Your *mother*?" The man rubs his face. "Your mother—did *she* drink bug juice?"

Sam nods. "She said once you had it, anything else was like *food.*" He laughs.

The man doesn't join him. "And did you . . . bring her to one of these places?"

Sam looks up and around the room. "Probably to this very one ten times, and to ten others ten times too." He glances at the salesman, and smiles at his horror. "Conveniences of the city. Back in Ohio you probably threw up in the privacy of your own toilet, right?"

"Right," says the man.

Sam nods. "I'm afraid we can't get Archie clean like this tonight. He's going to have to go dry out in white." Sam signals the salesman to lift the drunk, who groans and tries to roll to the floor.

"In white? I don't know what that means either."

They jack Archie up. He screams. "I know, buddy," says Sam. "Hurts in there." To the salesman he says, "In white means being checked into a treatment center. There's a minimum of four days drying out. It's not really long enough, but it gets them over *this.*"

They shuffle Archie out into the dark street, and turn toward the corner. The man says, "Did you finish these sessions by checking your mother into 'white'?"

Sam gives no sign of having heard. Just as the salesman starts to ask again, Sam says, "No. I never dried her out that way. Not for these quickies." He

swallows. "I always took her home. For these quickies."

The salesman doesn't ask anything else. People,
many of them drunk but not as drunk as Archie,
shout and jostle and laugh and scuffle on the sidewalk around them. Sam and the salesman take Archie to another brightly lit doorway, between the
doorways of a bar and a Mexican restaurant.

This is no large room smelling of eucalyptus. It is
a white cubicle with a short, chest-high counter, two
chairs, and a porcelain pot. Sam pushes Archie up to
the counter.

A young man in a white tunic as dirty as the walls
pushes a form across the counter. Sam begins to fill
it out. The man behind the counter glances at Archie
and rolls his eyes.

Sam nods. The man says, "Still got to test him,
though." Sam says, "Of course."

The man pulls from behind the counter a large
board, three feet square. On it is mounted an angular
mess of objects: colored disks on wires, grooved cyl-
inders with rods stuck in them, spiky balls that slide
over holes on nonparallel rails. The wood shows
through the chipped paint, the metal parts are rusted
and flaking, the edges of the board are splintered, and
the whole thing is spotted with stains. The man
shows it to Archie, points to a set of objects, and

139

gives him a complicated instruction. Archie's eyes are swollen shut from his broken nose, even though he now seems awake. He gives no response. The man points to another set of objects and gives more instructions; again Archie fails to move.

"We can skip the third test," the man says. Sam thanks him. The man hands him a plastic disk with a seven-digit number on it in blue ink. Another disk with the same number is tied around Archie's neck on a cloth-covered rubber cord. "Four days," says the man cheerily. "Pick him up. Call Central first."

"Any idea which center?"

"No idea," says the man.

"See if you can get him Foggy Bottom," says Sam. "Or Glover Park West. If possible."

The man raises his eyebrows and shrugs. Sam and the salesman go out onto the sidewalk. Two men appear and take Archie out the door and around the corner. A white station wagon is waiting. They sit Archie up in the backseat and fix him in a harness, with a canvas bag strapped over his mouth. They get in the front and drive away.

The salesman stares after the car. Sam pats him on the shoulder. "You going to be all right?" he says.

The man turns and looks at him. His eyes are wide in disbelief. "Yeah," he says. "Sure."

"You going to make it to Baltimore in the morning to sell them some carpet at that hospital?"

"Carpet," says the man. He looks after the car, which is gone. "Jesus Christ, carpet."

"Do you want me to get you a cab?" says Sam. "To the Ramada?"

"No," says the man, rubbing his face. "Don't worry. I'm okay." He stops rubbing and stares at Sam. "Would he be dead if I hadn't seen you?"

"No," says Sam. "You would have passed a sober bar and figured out to take him there. Or one of the attendants would have seen you pass and hustled you in. You'd have done all right."

The man shakes his head vaguely. He looks around the noisy street. "I can't believe you're . . . at *home* here," he says. "How old are you?"

Sam looks down the street. "There's a cab," he says. "If you don't want it, I do." He takes the man's hand in his and gives it a shake. "Thanks for helping Archie. A heck of a welcome to Washington." He smiles, and takes off. A moment later he turns. The man is still staring at him.

"What is it?" Sam says.

"He's . . . I met him in that group, and now he's alone," the salesman says. "It doesn't seem right. It was such a strong group. It doesn't seem right he's so alone right now."

"It's not a real group," says Sam. "It's a bunch of scared single people who stay together so they can watch it happen to somebody else first. I've worked there three years and I've seen dozens of them get drunk all of a sudden like this, after years of being clean. The only one who will go out and fetch some-one is Pepper, and he only does it in the daytime. At night he stays home and tries not to think about it happening to him."

"Oh," says the man.

"The one thing they all say is that you are alone when you get sober, and alone when you get drunk. They say it a lot. I used to think they were cold jerks, when one would get drunk and the others would talk about how they were all just solo guys. But I've seen it over the years. They're just being practical. Archie did this all by himself. If he sobers up, he'll do it the same way." Sam points at the man. "The way you did."

"I guess," says the salesman. "I guess I did."

"Keep it up," says Sam, turning away.

THURSDAY

F O U R T E E N

This is kind of delicate, Sam," says the man, pouring coffee into a mug sitting in front of the boy. "It's a very delicate thing we want to do here."

"Maybe it's better to say we don't want to *do* anything, really," says his wife, looking concerned. "This is just a little talk. We're not even asking anything. We just want to express a couple of things to you. For our peace of mind—just so we know you're aware of how we feel."

"We're not asking for anything, that's right," says the man.

Sam watches and listens politely, taking a sip of coffee.

"We obviously know the probation period ends tomorrow," says the man. "Now, of course, there is a ten-day period for the decision of, you know, whether to grant custody or to extend into a new probationary term, or to retain. We all know this. We're not hurrying, here. We've all got a lot to consider. Ten days isn't much time."

"We just thought it would be better to speak before it started than in the middle," says the woman anxiously. "We aren't expecting a decision right away. We should all be patient."

"You've been very patient for the past year," says Sam. "I know that better than anyone."

The man says, "Need some sugar in that coffee?"

"No, thanks."

"Okay," says the man, rubbing his hands. He walks over to his wife, and puts his arm around her shoulders. He looks at her, and she looks at Sam. "Basically," says the man, "we just want to let you know that we want Oliver."

"We remembered our counselor telling us it's supposed to be a probationary period for the foster parents to evaluate the child, as well as the other way," says the woman. "Though of course no one turns down a child these days, we just wanted to let you know, more or less formally, that from *our* side the probation has been a successful trial. We love Ollie and want him as our son. We can give him a good home."

"He's pretty useful for the nasty chores," says the man. "We think we'll keep him." He laughs. His wife looks at him in horror, but Sam laughs too.

When the laughter stops, Sam looks at them. "I'm glad you're taking the trouble of telling me this way," he says. "I assumed it, of course. But it's nice to hear. I mean, we've been in such close touch all the time that I think I know how you feel about Ollie." He thinks for a moment. "At times I've been afraid I placed so many restrictions on you that you couldn't really feel like parents. I'm pretty bossy, I know. I had a lot of demands."

"Well, you had a lot of responsibility. Really, your help made our adjustment to having a ten-year-old in the house much more *thorough*," says the woman. "We are so grateful for all of your—" She looks at her husband expectantly, then at Sam, but neither says anything. She shrugs. "I guess there's nothing to call it but 'supervision.' "

"There *is* one thing," says her husband. She looks at him with warning, but he shakes his head. He looks at Sam. "Well, frankly, the big deal about getting Ollie into a school where he would get a good education and no AO. There were times when it seemed almost like you would have been more in favor of one of the Steemer schools, just because they didn't have any AO, than one of the better private academies, because they did. We were all pretty lucky to come across Dunbarton, but for a while there I wondered." He shrugs. "What's the big deal with AO? Is it so terrible?"

Sam nods, then looks at the table for a few moments. The woman's face is drained of color and expression; she does not even risk a glare at her husband but stares at Sam, waiting. The man watches him too—easily, at first, but then, as the silence hangs, with a growing discomfort.

Sam does not look up. "I couldn't wait to start AO," he says softly, almost to himself. "I was in the third grade—it was the first year after the Epidemic legislation. We went to school on the first day, and the principal of the school told us about it in a special assembly. He made it sound so exciting; he told us it was the 'finest hour' for the schools of America, that the schools were taking the lead once more in the health of our society—and that we were being recognized once again as the most important people in the land."

Sam glances out the kitchen window. He does not look at the man or woman; they watch him and nothing else. "By 'we' I mean the schoolchildren," he says, "not the children of alcoholics. Because that was the thing—the Alcoholic Offspring program was something everybody in school had to take. Not just the kids whose parents were known to be drunks. That was the point, I guess. It seems like the Epidemic had surprised all the adults—all of a sudden they look around and seventy percent of them are alcoholics—and they were determined not to be surprised again. So they kind of made it clear that we could all expect *everyone* to turn into an alcoholic." Sam smiles wryly and shakes his head.

He pulls his coffee mug toward him and starts to lift it for a sip, but stops, and leaves it on the table. "My mother wasn't drinking yet. My father—well, the Epidemic had been one of the things that kind of started him burning with the big Christian rah-rah business, and he was always talking about alcoholism as the mark of the devil. So *he* wasn't drinking. But there I was, in AO, two periods a day, Theory and Doctrine one hour, and Problem Workshop the second hour." He is moving his mug slightly with both hands, watching it. "I was excited about being in this special program, with posters of a letter to *The Courageous Alcoholic Offspring* signed by the president, and newspaper reporters waiting to talk with us in the hallways after class. But"—he shakes his head, with a small smile—"I felt left out. My family didn't drink. They didn't seem as if they were *ever* going to drink. I didn't feel good about being safe like this; I felt *left out.*"

He glances at the man and woman, then back to his mug. "Up to then I had always been pretty much of a leader. You know, one of those kids who answers a lot of questions in class, or picks the teams on the playground and assigns positions and starts the ball game going. I liked always stepping up in front. I was pushy sometimes. My mother told me recently that I was a mean little Christian for a while, lecturing people and quoting the Bible and stuff. It doesn't surprise me; it was a way of putting myself up front." He smiles and raises his eyebrows. "I remember a word from the Meaningless List in one of the history books, a word they wore out in the late twentieth century: *innovator.* It meant someone who had new ideas and did things first. That was me. Until AO."

He is staring hard at the mug in his hands now. He waits a few moments. The man and woman do not shift, or sigh, or nod; they are as still as the walls.

"Every class began with a reading from the *AO Anthology,*" says Sam. "These were supposed to be 'case histories,' told straight and true. Later, of course, when kids were older and had heard the stories a few times and took a longer look at them, it was obvious they were told far from 'straight.' What a laugh they turned out to be. But when you are eight and you hear those horror stories for the first time—well, you don't ask if the style of writing is manipulative. You just listen, with your mouth open, and you believe every word. But you *can't* believe what you are hearing." He nods. "I remember. Our teacher, Miss Ashe, was a nonalcoholic. She was left out too, just like me. So she tried extra hard—she read the case histories every morning as if she had lived through every one. Or"—he smiles— "as if she had *died* through every one. Even then we thought her melodrama was kind of a joke—but it didn't matter. The stories were shocking, and fascinating, and we couldn't tear ourselves away."

He looks up at them, then down again. "At least some of us couldn't. The ones who *didn't* have alcoholic parents. The others . . . well, there was a kind of cool about them. They sat there and looked almost bored, paying just enough attention to show the stories simply confirmed what they already knew. What they already were living with. *Yes, sure, that's about how it is,* they seemed to be saying; *Yeah, big deal, I've seen that.*"

Sam shakes his head. "I didn't want to believe it. That this bouncy little guy beside me, or this smart happy girl in front of me, had been locked out of the house overnight in the winter, or left in the liquor store parking lot. It wasn't pity that made me want to doubt. It was envy. I was *jealous.*"

Sam looks up at the man and woman. His eyes are large, and seem darkened. He frowns slightly. The woman seems on the verge of moving toward him. But she doesn't. Sam stares at them. They wait.

"I was jealous," he says again.

He takes a deep breath. "Do you understand? I was jealous of the children who had alcoholic parents. I wanted—I wanted to be in there *with* them. I wanted the"—he makes a face of disgust—"the *glory.* I hated being out of it." He looks away, looks down at the table, closes his eyes.

"I wanted my mom to start drinking."

No one moves. Nothing ticks or creaks in the house. Sam seems to be close to a laugh. "I knew my dad was too far gone to be a good 'candidate.' He was already pretty ridiculous in his purity and evangelism; frankly, I kind of wished he would just get out of the way. So we could get on with the family tragedy that I was so ready to welcome. I wanted to be a good AO kid—a *star* AO kid. I was *prepared.* And Dad did it. One day he came home and said he was going off to save the Eskimos, and the next week he was gone." Sam looks up at them, and shrugs. "And a couple of months after that, I saw my mom drunk for the first time."

He speaks more rapidly now. "I came home from baseball practice after school. Ollie was at a day-care place, because my mom was supposed to be spending the days finding a job. I had a key. But when I unlocked the door, it didn't open. The chain was still on." He frowns. "It was very strange. I heard my mother inside talking on the telephone. I listened for a minute." He smiles oddly. "She was talking on the phone to *me.*"

"But—" says the man. His wife cuts him off with a gesture.

Sam nods. "Right. That's just what I said: 'But—' But she *was.* She kept calling me by name and yakking away. I listened to her. Her voice was thick and she couldn't pronounce certain sounds, and she was very agitated—one second she was saying sweet things to me on the phone and the next second she was *mean*, mean like she had never *really* been, like I had no idea she could be. Past her voice I could hear the recording on the telephone saying PLEASE RE-PLACE YOUR RECEIVER PLEASE REPLACE YOUR RE-CEIVER over and over again. It didn't bother my mother—she just kept talking."

The woman can't keep quiet any longer. "But what did you do?"

"I called her from the door." He pauses. "She wouldn't let me in."

"Of course not," says the man. "You were impersonating her kid."

"Right! Just what she said. She kept me locked out."

"And what about—"

"Ollie?" says the boy. "She was supposed to pick him up in only a couple of hours. I didn't know which center he had been left in, so I went to a pay telephone and spent the next day's lunch money calling day-care places. I found the right one on the third try." He smiles almost mischievously. "I imitated her voice. I told the person I was my mother, and would be sending my son Sam to pick Ollie up." He shrugs. "I went. I got him. It was easy—he wasn't but a little over three. I brought him home."

"How did you get in the house?" says the woman.

The man says, "Mom was ready."

Sam looks at him for a moment. "That's right. Ollie and I were walking up the sidewalk and I was trying to figure out how to get her to let us in without—you know, without him seeing her like that, and *shick* I heard the chain slide off, and out of the door stepped my mother, in a yellow dress, with makeup on—looking perfect. *Perfect.* She saw us, and stopped. Ollie waved or something, and went toward her. I stayed back. She smiled at Ollie, but then looked over his head at me. She just checked me out. I let her look, and I looked back. It was really her—she was okay now. She saw that I knew, and that was it." He lifts his hands simply, and drops them. "From then on, we had a secret."

No one speaks for a few moments. Then the man says, "So what you're telling us is that you kind of blame AO for making it . . . attractive?"

Sam glances at him. "No. I don't blame anybody but myself for that. But I just don't think learning a lot of theoretical terms does anybody any good." He shrugs. "It makes you believe you're going to be able to handle something you can't."

The woman smiles almost tenderly. Sam smiles back and gives a small nod. But the man makes no such sign; in fact, after a moment he says, "Sorry, Sam. I don't buy it."

The woman looks at him with disbelief. Sam frowns. "What do you mean?" he says coolly.

The man rubs his chin. "Well, I don't think that's why you want to keep Ollie away from AO. Mainly because I don't think you believe there's anything you can't handle."

Sam's lips are tight. "So?"

"So, I don't know, it rubs me wrong when you say that's the reason. And I look for another reason. And I come up with only one."

Sam watches him. "Only one."

"Right." The man nods. "I mean, it's your business, up to a point—and that point is the time Ollie becomes our son. If we are lucky enough to get him, and all that. My wife probably thinks I've blown everything by talking to you straight like this."

"Straight talk doesn't blow anything," Sam says grimly.

"Good. Then let's keep it up. Look—when we took Ollie into our home, you told us absolutely no AO, and you said Ollie was too shy about it to share the experiences he'd been through with his mom with any 'strangers.' Meaning kids in AO class, and meaning us."

"Sorry I called you that," says Sam. "I meant—"

"I know what you meant," says the man, holding up a hand. "We *were* strangers. We are not strangers now. But I bet if we brought up the subject of alcoholism with Ollie now . . . Well, let me put it to *you.* Would he run weeping from the room?"

Sam, holding the man's eye, quietly says, "No."

"Would he run weeping into our arms?"

"No."

"Okay, then. Would he stare at us blankly? And maybe say 'What?' in that blinky way he has?"

Sam lets a long breath out through his nose. With his lips tight, he nods.

"Wait." The woman looks from her husband to Sam. "What are you saying? Either of you."

The man says, "Sam is saying Ollie doesn't *know* his mom's an alcoholic." He puts his arm around his wife's shoulders and looks at her. "He's saying he thinks he's kept it away from Ollie. He *and* his mom, I guess." He looks at Sam. "What was it you said? 'We had a secret'?"

The woman looks at Sam. She shakes her head. "Sam?"

"It's true," he says.

"Sam, I can't believe you'd tell us—"

"Ollie doesn't know."

"—all this time—"

"It was my decision a long time ago, and I stand by it."

"—such a *lie*, Sam. Such a big, big, big, big lie. I mean—what if—"

"I explained to you that you should never bring it up. As long as you followed my directions, nothing would go wrong. It doesn't matter what reasons I gave, as long as you listened. And you have. And

157

nothing *is* wrong. So no more talk about lies, please."

The husband says, "I don't think Sam *did* tell us a lie, anyway."

His wife looks at him and says impatiently, "You didn't follow. He said—"

"He said Ollie knew and was too shy to talk about it." He nods at her, then looks over at Sam. "I think there's nothing wrong with that. In fact, I kind of think it's right on the money."

Sam looks wary. "What do you mean?"

The man lifts his shoulders and lets them fall. "Ollie knows."

"Has he said anything that you've kept from me?" Sam asks sharply.

"Far from it," says the man easily. "Far, far from it. He's said nothing. He's been as clean as you believe he thinks his mom is. Where *does* he think she is, anyway?"

"In a hospital. With a . . . disease. That was enough for him."

"Sure," says the man.

Sam is frowning. "He couldn't know, really. You couldn't be right."

"It sure would mess up your scheme of things, whatever that is."

"What do you mean by *that*?"

"Something's going on, Sam. You aren't cruising up to this custody-date business with the casual, matter-of-fact attitude you're showing. Anybody who knows you would know it, son—you just don't do big things that way. Now, it's still your show—for a few more days. For a few more days you can hold all the cards. I don't lie awake worrying about what you're doing; you're too smart for me, and I mean that. I only worry about keeping Oliver happy. I figure if we do that, we just have to count on you to come through and see it, no matter what tricks you pull for everybody else. So we're not asking you to fill us in. We know from the counselor—we called him; that's our right—that you asked him five weeks ago to have the custody papers ready for transfer by tomorrow. We hope that means we're neck and neck at the wire. That's enough for us." He smiles slightly. "I don't know who we're neck and neck with—but I have an idea."

"I'd better go now," says Sam, moving to the door.

"Wait a minute, son."

Sam waits.

The man says, "I said you hold the cards. I said we aren't asking to see them. But I do ask one thing—or, better yet, I *say* it." He points a solid finger in Sam's direction. "You be sure this scheme of yours doesn't leave us with a broken boy. You be aware that you are playing with a *life*, here."

"I'm not playing," Sam says. "I don't play with people."

"More's the pity," says the man.

F I F T E E N

Ollie, alone and blinking, walks rapidly by Sam, who is waiting beside a tree off the school's front walk. Sam's expectant smile fades momentarily as it becomes clear Ollie is passing, but he fixes it again and darts after the younger boy.

"Ollie!"

Ollie turns. He peers. "Oh. Hi, Sam."

"You walked right by me," says Sam, grinning. "Some pal *you* are."

Ollie looks around. "Where were you?"

"Standing under that tree."

"Oh," says Ollie. "Yeah. I thought you were just some guy."

Sam looks closely at him and says, "Are you seeing okay in school? Any problem when you sit in the back of the class? Maybe it's time to get some new glasses. You get headaches?"

"No, I'm okay," says Ollie. He shrugs. "You just looked like, you know, some guy to me. Some man I didn't know. I'm not used to seeing you here. You usually work."

They begin to walk away from the school. "Yeah, well, Mr. Culpepper gave me some time off. I *do* have to get back soon, though, so I'll get right down to it. I came," he says merrily, "to make an appointment with you."

"An appointment? For what? New glasses?"

"No, not for anything like that."

"I thought appointments were only for the doctor and stuff."

"It's just a word, Ollie. I want to take you somewhere tomorrow after school, and I want you to save some time for it. I want to make sure you will be here, and meet me, and come."

Ollie says nothing. They walk. Sam clears his throat to repeat himself, but Ollie says, "Okay."

"Okay," says Sam. They walk on for a while. Ollie doesn't say anything; he doesn't even look sideways at his brother, who keeps looking expectantly at him. After a couple of blocks, Sam says, "Hey, come *on*, Ol."

"What?"

"Aren't you . . . you know, curious about where I'll be taking you for our appointment?"

"No," says Ollie. "As long as it's not the doctor, I don't care."

Sam shakes his head. Then he says, "Well, I'll tell you anyway. You remember Mom went into the hospital?"

"Sure," says Ollie. "She had some disease."

"She's out," says Sam with a huge, silent sigh.

Ollie looks at him, slowing down. He says, "Is she fixed? Is her disease gone?"

"Well," says Sam, "not exactly. Not completely." He thinks. "It's a disease that you never get completely over. But she's much better."

"I thought all those diseases got fixed," says Ollie. "They got rid of all of them back after the twentieth century. That's what we heard in health class."

"Not this one," says Sam. "But let's talk about Mom being *better.*"

"Oh," says Ollie. "Okay."

But Sam says nothing; he thinks as they walk for a block.

"Ollie."

"Yeah."

"You . . . did you like Mom? Did you like it when the three of us lived together?"

Ollie looks at him briefly. "Sure," he says.

"You don't have to say yes just because she's your mother," Sam says. "Or because she's *my* mother. I mean, I'm just really interested in how you feel about it. About how it was with the three of us."

Ollie thinks. "It was okay," he says.

"It was okay," Sam repeats. "And 'okay' means . . . what? 'Pretty good'?"

"Sure," says Ollie. "It was pretty good, I guess."

Sam waits, but nothing more is coming. He says, "And what about living with the Bigelows? How is *that*?"

"Pretty good," says Ollie.

"Right," says Sam. He shakes his head slightly again. They walk. Sam looks at Ollie several times, but Ollie says nothing more. After a while Sam too puts his head down and plods in silence.

They come to the avenue on which Sam's bus runs. Sam sits down on a wall. Ollie stops too.

"You can go ahead," says Sam, with a listless wave. "Bye."

"Bye," Ollie says, but he doesn't move away. He looks around for a few moments. He watches Sam, who seems for once to be oblivious, with his chin in his hands, staring at the middle of the street. Ollie says, "Sam?"

"Yes?" He doesn't look up.

"Does Mom *want* to see me? I mean—did she, you know, like *demand* to see me or something?"

Sam comes to life immediately, standing up, starting to gesture. "Well," he says, "I mean, absolutely. She . . . *demanded* it, the minute she got out. It was me who held things up. I just—well, I thought we'd do it tomorrow, mainly for—"

"I just wondered if I *have* to."

Sam stops. "Have to?"

"Yeah. If I *have* to see her right now."

"If you— What would you rather do? Skip it?"

Ollie shrugs. "I don't know." He watches Sam. Sam says nothing. Ollie makes a light gesture. "I guess it's okay. If she asked and stuff, I guess I better. Okay." He nods and smiles. "See you tomorrow." He starts to walk away.

"Wait, Ollie," says Sam. Ollie turns around. Sam

studies him. "Is there some reason you *don't* want to see Mom?"

"No," says Ollie. When Sam continues to wait, he adds, "Some of the kids were going to kick the ball around, is all."

Sam rolls his eyes. "Oh," he says. He laughs. "That's all—kicking a ball around? There's no other reason you have for avoiding it?"

"No," says Ollie. "That's all."

"Then you should come," says Sam.

"Okay," says Ollie. "I will."

*　　*　　*

"Sure," says Mr. Culpepper, "take as much time as you like."

"Only tomorrow," says Sam. "It will be the last day off I need. I really appreciate it. You've been very understanding this week. Now it's over, almost. Things will be back to normal on Monday."

Culpepper studies him, and lights a cigarette. "You seem pretty sure about that."

Sam takes a deep breath. "Well," he says, "I guess I am. I mean, they *have* to be."

Culpepper nods, looks at the press running beside him. "If you need more time off, you can take it." He looks back at Sam. "The only thing you can be sure of with a drunk is that you can't be sure."

Sam laughs. "Why, Mr. C., that's straight from the Second Doctrine! I never knew you took AO."

Culpepper grunts, and looks back at his press. "I didn't," he says. "I just spend every day around drunks."

"So do I," says Sam.

"Then you ought to know better," says Culpepper.

* * *

"Well," says Sam's mother, wiping her mouth neatly, "I suppose I better skip the brandy and head home. Big day tomorrow, eh?"

"Yes," says Sam, pushing a piece of broccoli for a last circuit around his full plate and putting his fork down. "Big."

"What's wrong?" says his mom. "I would think you'd be excited—the impresario before opening night, and all that."

"How can you joke?" he says, looking up at her sharply. "I would think it's the biggest decision of your life."

"How could it be?" she says. "It's not a decision

I'm even *making*. It's more like the biggest decision of *your* life, or at least it looks as if that's how you see it."

"How do you see it?"

She shrugs. "As something else that's out of my hands."

"That's all?" Sam nearly slams his napkin down. "God, how selfish."

She smiles oddly. "If letting somebody else take all the initiative from your life is selfish, I stand accused. Me, I'm just a girl who goes along with the law."

Sam, leaning over his plate, has picked up a spoon, and takes a chop at a vegetable. "I suppose you're implying that the selfish one is me. Well, believe me, I'm not doing any of this for myself."

"No, but you're doing it all your *way.*" She looks at him, reaches over, and pulls his chin up until he looks at her. "Maybe that's the ultimate selfishness. Maybe that's worse than simply taking care of yourself and letting others do the same."

"I already let you take care of yourself, for years," he says.

She sits back with a smile. "Oh, were you 'letting' me do all that? Thanks, Sambo. And all this time I thought I was getting drunk on my own—to think, you were managing me in my darkest hours."

He sighs, drops his spoon into his plate, and signals a waiter for the check. "You're ridiculous," he says. "You're a child."

"You're ridiculous too," she says. "You're *not.*"

He glares at her, eyes flashing. The waiter, seeing Sam's expression, turns away quickly and vanishes back into the kitchen. The woman watches him go and says to Sam, "Calm down, honey, you're frightening the help." Then, in a softer voice, she adds: "I'm sorry, Sambo. I know I haven't given you the chance to have a childhood."

Sam continues to burn at her. Finally he says, "I *am* a child. Therefore this *is* a childhood. It may not look like it to you and all the other people who tell me what a little man I am. Well, this is not being a man—this is what *children* do nowadays."

He takes a breath, sags a little. When he speaks again, his voice is softer. "It's *okay*, though. That's what nobody understands. People think, *You poor kid, your life stinks.* Well—my life *doesn't* stink. I make sure it doesn't." He takes a deep breath. "How do you think it feels to have everybody telling you you're pitiful, when you're just *living*?" He sets his jaw. "I like my life. I do a good job of it."

"Oh, how can you like it, Sam?" his mother says, in a pleading voice. "How can you like holding your babbling mommy up by the head while you look for the contents of her purse in a trash can on the sidewalk—where she dumped it—and one of your teachers walks by? Remember that? That wasn't something you could like. When I think back and try, I can't think of anything . . ." She cannot finish. She looks down.

He puts his hand across the table. "No, it's *okay*. I mean, it's not exactly fun but—" He stops sharply. She looks up. He looks terrified.

"Say it," she says.

He shakes his head. "Say it," she says.

He can barely keep his eyes on hers. In a small voice he finishes his sentence: ". . . but it's not going to kill me."

She nods. "Meaning it *is* going to kill *me*. That's what you're saying." She shakes her head and laughs slightly. "Boy, you have a way of hitting some great points, Sam."

"But it's true," he says. "It's the reason I can never feel sorry for *me*. Doesn't it sound stupid—'My mother is killing herself with alcohol; pity poor *me*.' "

"Yeah, well, don't pity poor me too fast either." She reaches up and touches his face. "I'm here, aren't I? For as long as you keep me here. To tell you the truth, *that's* a decision I have my eye on more than one about Ollie."

"They're the same," he says.

"They shouldn't be," she says. "But I'll take what I can get."

S I X T E E N

The doorway is dark, but as the cardinal knocks for a third time he sees a dim light begin to show through the cracks around the door. He stops knocking. The light stops coming. He knocks again, and the light advances. Finally, the door opens, and Prior Marloe peers around the edge, holding a candle.

"Yes?" he says cautiously. "Oh. Your Grace."

"Good evening, Jack. I was . . . more or less out this way, and because I thought I might be passing

I brought along some things I thought perhaps you could use." He hoists a bulky canvas bag. "One of our members recently donated a replacement set of Bibles to our Sunday school." He laughs. "We could have better used a few other things, like drywall for the sacristy or new slate for the apse roof, but . . ." He hands the canvas bag to Marloe, who reaches out from inside to take it.

"Thank you," says Marloe, frowning. He hefts the bag indecisively.

"You *do* use Scripture, don't you, prior? I hadn't thought of the possibility that you'd have come up with new texts in so short a time—"

"Yes, yes, of course I do," says Marloe. "I'm sorry. Very nice. Very grateful—of course we can make use of these. Yes. Thanks."

The cardinal waits, watching Marloe, who still looks at the bag and frowns. Their breath makes yellow clouds in the cold candlelight.

"And how is the problem we discussed a few days ago? The acolyte?"

Marloe looks up sharply. "Oh," he says. "Well— no better, I'm afraid. In fact, he's here. Right now. It's why I'm not asking you in." He shakes his head. "He's been here every night this week. Nearly every night for a month."

"You'll pardon me for mentioning it, but I shouldn't think it was a good place for a boy to come at night. I'm surprised at his parents."

"He . . . I think he lies to them. He always has a music case or an athletic bag. I believe he pretends to have some sort of sanctioned activity."

"You haven't inquired? I suppose it's a delicate thing with a congregation of children: How much do you leave alone? How much do you treat them as adults? A terribly delicate matter."

"I hardly have the opportunity to speak," says Marloe, looking harried. He looks at the cardinal, glances behind him, steps out onto the porch a bit more, pulling the door almost closed behind him. He lowers his voice now, speaking rapidly. "He—this is a bitter child, and he spends his time here expressing his bitterness. In the most . . . exhaustive condemnations. I'm certain he's come to me from another church, possibly several other churches—he has a command of the Steemer rhetoric that is appalling." Prior Marloe smiles grimly.

"Why do you smile?"

"Because I think he has come to me in anticipation of a *harsher* rhetoric. The Steemers were too *tame* for him, I think. All he seems to have absorbed from one of my sermons is that I am especially sympathetic to the children of alcoholics. The *angle* of my alertness he has missed entirely—he simply assumes I go further than anyone in condemning parents who drink! Can you imagine!"

The cardinal studies him, nodding slowly. "Well, Jack, I told you it was a . . . terribly *subtle* kind of message you wished to bear. Especially in light of the age group you anticipated for your congregation." He sighs. "Alas, it is easier to preach good and evil. The early apostles were wise in many areas, not the least of them practicality."

Marloe's eyes flare for an instant. "Yes, certainly, Your Grace. Good and evil. Well, if ever a human being demonstrated the inadequacy of artificially simple judgments, it is this child. The simplistic Steemer doctrine has tied him in knots." He sighs. "God knows what my 'subtle' doctrine would do, if I could even get it across to him."

The cardinal nods, raises his eyebrows sympathetically, and pulls his coat tighter around him. He places a hand on Marloe's arm. "I should leave you to your charge," he says. "I'm certain you have been given this particularly unanticipated challenge as a kind of grace, Jack. It *is* different from a doubting heckler or a zealous apostle, isn't it? You'll do fine with him, my boy. But—" He frowns.

"What is it?"

The cardinal looks into the street. "I would find

some way of informing his parents. Or, of course, if they are alcoholic and liable to misinterpretation, of checking with his teachers. You really are taking on a lot, when you assume so much from children. I believe I noted this at one of our debates about your mission. You *do* want to give them *so* much rein, Jack."

Marloe sets his jaw. "They can handle it," he says. "This child is . . . just a unique case."

"I believe God would have us think they all are," says the cardinal. "I hope you can handle *that*. Good night, Prior Marloe."

He leaves the porch. The door closes behind him, and the light fades quickly.

FRIDAY

S E V E N T E E N

O llie is waiting beneath the tree. Sam opens the door of the taxi and waves. Ollie sees him right away and comes, carrying his saxophone case but no books.

"Hi," says Ollie.

"You going to play something for Mom?" says Sam. "What a great idea."

Ollie looks at him. "I don't know, maybe."

Sam puts his arm around Ollie and gives him a squeeze. "You do whatever you're comfortable doing. I'm sure Mom would love a song or two. But of course she wouldn't want you to force yourself."

"Sure," Ollie says. "Of course."

The cab moves quickly across town. "I thought we'd pick her up at work," says Sam. "She's been working in a dress shop. I arranged with her boss for her to get off early today; she doesn't know about it. It'll be kind of a surprise." He looks at Ollie, then back out the window. "I thought we'd kind of catch her *fresh* that way. Instead of going to her place after she's come home from work."

"Sure," says Ollie.

"People get home from work, they're all alone, sometimes they're not as . . . fresh."

"Right," says Ollie.

They roll along. The cab turns into light traffic, makes its way down busy streets; the boys do not speak, though Sam seems on the verge of saying something several times. Finally, after a turn, he says, "This is the block. We're almost there."

Ollie nods.

The driver mutters something, stops short; Sam leans forward. "What's the matter?" he says.

"I don't know, something happening," says the driver. He gestures ahead. Two police cars are stopped in the street, one with the top light revolving slowly. A crowd on the sidewalk has strayed into the road. Loud voices rise from behind the crowd.

Sam strains to see. His face goes white. "That's the shop," he says. "That's—" He looks at Ollie. "Stay here," he says. He opens the door. "I'll be back," he says to the driver. "Please wait."

"Sure thing," says the man. Sam is already running to the crowd.

He winds his way through two dozen people to the sidewalk in front of the store. The owner is standing there, gesturing frantically and speaking in a near shriek. Next to her one policeman nods and takes notes in a small notebook. Another policeman keeps trying to catch her arm gently, but every time he gets a light grasp she flails it into another wild arc to emphasize a point.

Behind her, the front window of the shop has been shattered by a mannequin thrown from the inside. It is dressed hideously—thick plaid pants beneath a silk paisley skirt, four blouses put on backward, scarves tied around the eyes and mouth, and a stocking worn as a droopy hat. It lies now with its face on the sidewalk, its torso angling upward through the jagged edges of the window, its legs skewed into the shop.

"You!" shrieks the woman. She has spotted Sam. The policemen look up in alarm. Sam steps forward.

The woman runs at him, stops just short of a collision. She waves her hands around him, as if to decide where to grab. He frowns at her. "What happened?" he says.

"What happened!" she yowls. "What happened!" She turns to the police, who are walking over. "Can you believe this? He asks 'What happened?' like a sweet little child."

Sam says, "Where is my mother?"

"Is this the boy?" one policeman asks the woman; the other nods with noncommittal politeness to Sam. Sam says to him, "What happened?"

"Seems a lady kind of went on a spree," the policeman says.

"Spree! A spree is when you come into my shop and *buy* things," screams the owner. "This! This is a drunken *rampage*!"

Sam says, "Drunken." He grabs the woman by the upper arms. "Did— Was my mother drunk? Are you sure? How do you know?"

The woman looks at him close up, then leans back in his grasp. "Look at that! He's afraid I've upset the sad dear woman who tore my business apart!" She laughs wildly.

"Now, now," says one policeman. "Let's calm down. Enough of that, okay?" He takes her firmly a few steps away as his partner guides Sam in the other direction.

When they stop, Sam asks, "How long ago did this happen?"

"She called us twenty minutes ago," the policeman says. "Now what was your name and address, sir?"

Sam gives it. As the policeman writes, Sam asks, "Was there any evidence that my mother—any evidence of drunkenness?"

"I'd say so, sir," says the policeman, looking at his pad as he writes. "We discovered two empty pint bottles of brandy in a dressing room. And the lady's apparent behavior indicates a certain condition, sir. Now—the lady is a guardian of yours?"

Sam nods. The man writes. The other policeman has walked the owner, hollering, back into the shop.

"And your mother as well, sir?"

Sam nods.

"And where may we locate the lady, sir?"

"She's staying with me. She's just out of Soberlife. She's been staying with me for a few days until we see if . . . if it works out."

The policeman says, "Sorry, sir."

Sam says, "Thanks."

The policeman says, "And would this be the address, sir?"

"Yes," says Sam. "Listen—if you head over

there, I'll meet you; I have my younger brother with me in that taxi." The policeman glances over. Sam says, "He hasn't seen her since she was released a few days ago. This was to be their reunion. He's been in a foster home. I'd rather not take him straight over where my mother is, if you know what I mean. . . ."

"I understand, sir." The policeman frowns and thinks, tapping his notebook with his pen. "You simply want to drop the youngster at his foster residence?"

Sam nods.

"And then you'll proceed to this address?"

"Right," says Sam.

The policeman nods, thinks, taps. He looks up. "All right. Customarily we would ask you to accompany us, but . . ."

"Thanks," says Sam. "I'll leave now, and meet you immediately."

He dashes back to the cab.

"Drive back the way we came," he tells the driver. "But then turn down L street and go to Mass Ave. and we'll head over to Dupont Circle." The driver backs up and turns around.

"What happened?" says Ollie, sitting still with his case on his lap. "Where's Mom?"

"At her house, I think," says Sam. "Ollie—she

might be kind of . . . sick today. I haven't got time to run you home, so I'm going to stop at her apartment and have the driver take you after—"

"No," says Ollie.

"What—?"

"I'm coming," Ollie says.

Sam looks at him hard. "Ollie," he says, "it—when Mom is sick, she—it's just not very—"

"I'm coming."

Sam looks at him there, sitting simply, feet together, sax case on his knees; Sam's eyes fill with tears. He reaches over and pulls Ollie to him.

"You want to help her, don't you, Ol? You love her and you just want to be there to help her, right? You're good, Ollie. You're just a good kid. A good son. A really good son, Ollie."

Ollie says nothing. They ride.

* * *

Sam asks the driver to wait, and they run up the stairs. The reek of alcohol has crept down to meet them. When they reach the landing, Sam sees the burgundy door is open.

Sam hesitates, then strides into the room. "Mother?" he says loudly. He looks automatically to the front, and sees quickly that the painting of the

185

window has changed: the cactus has been crudely painted into a shack, with a big sign saying TAVERN in red letters.

"Like the view?" says a voice from the back of the room. He turns, just as Ollie walks in behind him and turns as well.

She is sitting sideways in a chair, with her legs cocked over one of its arms. A low black shoe hangs from the toes of one foot, but she does not dangle it—it hangs still and straight, as if forgotten. Her hands rest on her stomach, where they hold a glass half full of a clear, amber liquid. A bottle of it is open on a table. Her face, turned toward them, is brilliant everywhere except the eyes: the cheeks shine pink, the mouth glistens in a smile, the eyebrows arch energetically. The eyes, despite a high sheen and a jaunty cheeriness, seem thick and opaque.

When she sees Ollie, though, the dullness vanishes. She stands up alertly, the shoe dropping. For a moment it seems she will walk crisply to where Ollie stands; but after staring at him for a second her eyes go dull again, her tautness sags. She falls back into the chair, slings her legs over the arm, resumes her old position exactly. She lifts a hand. "Hi, Ollie," she says. "Long time no see." Her voice is dull at the center, with exaggerated expressiveness at the edges. Ollie does not say anything.

Both of the boys stare.

"Fine thing," she says. "Mom comes home from work. Cold room. Desert painted on the wall. No food, no loving. Would you like a desert painted on your wall, Oliver? No. Does she get a hug? Hasn't seen him in eighteen months in prison."

"You were in the hospital," says Sam involuntarily.

"Schmospital," she says. "They don't torture you in the hospital, do they? Make you read books about what a mess you are? Learn big words. Write essays. 'How Drunk Mom Screws Up Everybody Through Post-Intake Counter-Exhilaration Aggressivity.'" She slows down for the long words but gets them right. She smiles. "Got all A's, my boys. Eligible for parole."

"You're *drunk*," says Ollie, as if he has never heard the word before.

His mother hesitates for an instant, eyes sinking; but then with a breath she nods enthusiastically. "Right. And *a* drunk. Two ways. Drunk and *a* drunk. Time we faced it, right? *A* drunk means it happens a lot. Don't worry, though. Sambo will handle it for you. No trouble at all." She turns her head to take a long swallow from the glass, her throat moving.

Sam hears a noise and turns toward Ollie. Ollie has

opened his saxophone case, assembled the instrument, and taken an odd leaning stance so that its bell points aggressively at his mother. The mouthpiece is in his mouth; he takes a sharp breath, and blows.

The notes are piercing and loud. They tumble out of the bell like people fleeing a fire, but there is a rough rhythm to them. Ollie's eyes burn at his mother above his bulging cheeks; he watches her without a blink through every squawk and bleat. She sits flush against the back of her chair, as if blown flat by the sound, staring blankly. Ollie glares, blows harder, hits a cadence and keeps it, one two one two one two, wild honks sawing through the room. He bobs slightly with the effort; no one else moves. The saxophone's honks change to even louder squeals, animal but metallic, like the howl of a wounded robot. Ollie's face is dark red as he blows, and blows, eyes white and fixed, until at last he peels back with a gasp from a shrieking note that seems to climb even after he has stopped.

Sam shivers. His mother, shaking her head almost imperceptibly, watches with a frown. Ollie, panting less, speaks in a voice thickening with melodrama.

"And it came to pass that all those upon this earth whom Satan had marked, in their weakness, for his own, were set one test of redemption." He shakes the saxophone. "One test! They were set the choice of taking the wine only in its holiness, and *resisting its temptations* at all other times! Or"—Ollie's voice drops to a mock growl—"they were suffered to steal its darkness unto themselves, and harbor it, and grow in weakness among us—for the service of *evil.*"

His face twists in a grimace; he moves toward his mother but stops. He stares uncertainly, panting again, his lips moving with unheard words. He takes a step, then stops; he begins to speak, but sputters. And then, with a groan that sounds more helpless than fierce, he swings the heavy saxophone behind his head, and hurls it at the woman. She cries out and throws her arms up, but it catches her a spinning blow. Ollie jumps back, and looks around. He flinches when he sees Sam begin to move toward him, jumps past the older boy, and runs through the open door. The steps rattle; the front door slams; an engine starts, and moves off. It is a matter of seconds, and Ollie is gone. Sam stands and stares out past the burgundy door.

A voice behind him says, "Nice to see the spirit of the Lord just keeps flowing in this family."

Sam turns. She is sitting forward, her hands over the top of her head. They are bloody.

Sam takes two steps toward the door. He turns to his mother again, then looks back at the door.

"Chase him if you like," says the woman, without

looking up. "But if you're going to stay here, relax. I'm getting a headache and I don't need you shuffling and fidgeting."

Sam looks a last time through the door, and then says, "Mother." He raises his hands and lowers them.

"I can feel the cut," she says. "It's not much. He raised a little skin here at the top. Thick hair saved the day."

"Yes," says Sam.

She looks up at him. "Sit down," she says. "But first hand me a towel."

He goes mechanically and gets a towel from the bathroom, and hands it to her. He sits in the other chair. She flicks a look at him as she dabs her wound with a towel end, then wraps the towel around her head like a turban. He frowns, looking straight ahead.

She tucks the ends of the towel together behind her neck, and leans back. She frowns briefly at her fingers, rubs them together, and puts her hands on the arms of the chair.

"Well, they told us those churches had made great strides in the past couple of years," she says. "But I take it you're as surprised as I am that they've started raiding the fifth grade for converts."

Sam glances at her. "Yes," he says. "Yes. I didn't know." He wrinkles his forehead and rubs his hands over his face a couple of times, slowly. After a few moments, he says, "Practice."

"What?"

"Practice. He was going to church when he said he had practice for sports, or band rehearsal. That must be it. It couldn't be any other time. I *know* the Bigelows wouldn't take him to one of those churches. They know how I feel about it; I insisted he be in a nonaffiliated school. I tried. I really did. He must have . . ." He blinks, then rubs his face again.

"Don't worry about it. Ollie's a cute one, sly enough to be invisible. Always has been. Not like you at all. He gets it from me."

"Ollie's not sly," Sam says, with a sudden anger, "and you can't shift the blame by criticizing him. Look what *you've* done!" He sweeps his hand around the room. It is strewn with discarded clothing; the sheets are twisted off the bed; one curtain is looped over the rod. In a voice that billows with indignation he says, "I just can't *believe* you could blow it like this. I can't believe—it goes beyond weakness, or even illness—" He looks at her. "I was offering you your boy. I didn't expect you to stay sober forever—just to stay sober in front of *him.*" He stares at her. She stares back, coolly. He groans, and puts his head in his hands. "How could you?" he says. "How could you not do everything possible to keep your boy?"

She looks at him evenly. " 'My boy,' " she says. "You say it with such devotion. What makes you so sure I feel that way just about Ollie?"

Sam sputters. "He—you—you're his—"

"I'm his mother, yes. But am I anybody else's? It's a tough question—take your time before you answer."

Sam is confused. "What are you talking about?"

She sits back, looking at the mural. "I'm talking about my boy. *My* boy." She looks at him. "I'm talking, perhaps, about doing 'everything possible' to keep the only boy *I* could really have."

Sam looks wary. "I don't understand. You could have had Ollie. I was *offering* him to you."

She shakes her head. "I've *never* had Ollie. I never really could; no one could, not even you, no matter how much you loved him. You ask how I could blow it today. The fact is, I blew it for Ollie a long time ago. By drinking, yes, and by all the things that happen to feelings and understanding. Don't fool yourself. Ollie's been on his own longer than you have."

"How can you just *say* that? How can you act like you accept it? If it's true, he *needs* so much, and even

192

in your condition, even . . . such as you are, how can you act like this when your child needs you. . . ."

She lets him sputter out. Then she says. "Maybe both of my children need me. And maybe I have to choose between them. So I choose the one who needs me more. Such as I am."

"You seem to be talking about me," Sam says. "It's not a funny joke."

"I only joke when I know I'm going to lose something," she says. "It's a way of getting ready. I've been getting ready to lose Ollie for years now—don't you see that? Don't you see how I couldn't help but know he was going to be taken away from me? I knew it when I first started; I knew it that first time, when you came home with him and he ran up to me on the sidewalk. I think that's why I protected him, right from the beginning—I knew one day he'd be out of it."

She watches Sam; he doesn't move. "I'm not going to lose *you*," she says. "Not now. I'll fight for what I want this time."

He cannot get it. "Want?"

"Sam. Look. I have put us all through a lot of trouble. More will follow, surely. But Ollie has room to maneuver. He will be okay. We couldn't help much even if we were there all the time for him."

She squeezes his hands. "Instead I have to think about what you need, and what I want. I want my boy."

Sam says, "You want me? Alone?"

"You wouldn't be alone," she says. "I'm here too. We'd be together."

"Without Ollie?"

"Without Ollie." She says it with great definition. He looks at the floor, frowning. She watches him, then says, "You are my son. *My* son." She smiles, and says more softly, "Ollie would always be more like *yours.*"

He looks at the floor for a long time, thinking. Then, looking her in the eye, he says, "Tell me something."

She smiles tenderly. "Anything."

He says, "Are you really drunk?"

She meets his eyes, and says nothing. He disengages his hands, and gets up. He walks over to the table where the bottle of amber liquid sits. He looks back at her as he picks it up.

"Don't," she says.

Looking at her the whole time, he tilts the bottle to his mouth and takes a swallow. He lowers it.

"Flat cola and water," he says. He points at her. "You had to plan this—you had to let the cola go flat." He shakes his head. "Why? I can see acting sober when you're drunk. But why put on an act that would *blow* everything?"

She says, "Before we talk about that, it's time for *you* to confess something."

He looks a little wary. "What?"

"If I had been sober today—smiling, dressed in silk, smelling of rosewater—if I had been perfect, would you have handed Ollie over to me? Really?"

He looks at the table. "Well . . ."

"Was it all *really* at stake here, today? Was this really a test, with Ollie as the prize? Would you have ripped him out of that nice foster home, and stuck him here with me? Even in silk? Even with all the promises I could make?"

He handles the bottle. "I intended to," he says. "I intended to set it up that way. I would bring him by, the two of you would fall into each other's arms— and my choice would be easy. You'd have something to live sober for, he'd have the true parent at her best. The Bigelows would lose out, but . . . that's the chance they took."

"This, as you say, was what you *intended*," she says. He nods. She says, "But what did you actually *do*?"

Sam suddenly raises a hand to his mouth. "Oh

God," he says. "I didn't even *tell* him. He ran out before—"

"Tell him *what*? What have you done?"

Sam shakes his head. "I signed him over to the Bigelows last night, and left the papers in their mailbox this morning."

They look at each other. His expression is fearful; hers is stark.

"Ollie," she says. "Ouch."

"Mother . . ."

"It kind of hits you when it's a fact. Getting ready is fine, knowing the custody law and all that, but . . . Whew." Her eyes fill with tears, but she doesn't cry. "He really *is* gone."

Sam watches her. "I'm sorry," he says. "I had to do something. I had to decide, I—"

"It's all right." She looks at him. "I just need to sit here and feel it for a moment."

Sam stares at the floor, almost writhing, but silent. When his mother finally looks up and says, "It's okay, Sam," he shivers and holds his hands out to her.

"I had to do something," he says. "I had to, for Ollie's sake. I couldn't tell—I thought you really didn't care. I saw the whole thing clearly last night, and I was afraid I'd change my mind today if I let it go until you saw each other and liked each other. . . ." He pleads with her: "You always *joked* about him, you teased me about him, you didn't want to see him that first day—"

"I wanted to see you first," she says. "You should have thought of that, Sam. You should have known I love you."

"But . . ." He cannot go on. He stands there, almost frantic. She gets up easily, and puts her arms around him from behind.

"It's okay," she says.

He gestures, moves his mouth wordlessly.

"It's *all right*," she says, rocking him slightly. "What you did—setting Ollie up with his fosters—it's what I was doing *for* you, today. Don't you see? I said last night that it wasn't my decision, that you had kept it all to yourself. I realized later I *did* have a way to make the decision. All by myself." She hugs him closer. "I did it, Sam. You aren't the only one responsible. Even if you signed the papers beforehand, I did this."

Sam, still not leaning back into her, nods uncertainly. After a moment, he finds a small voice and says, "May I ask one more thing?"

"Sure."

He waits, making sure of his voice. He says, "If

you protected Ollie—never drinking in front of him—and you say you loved me all this time too . . . then why did you *never* protect *me?*" He pulls himself away, and turns, and looks at her. "How could I know—how could I expect you to feel like this about me? You want *me?* You got *drunk* in front of me!"

Frowning deeply, she takes him back in her arms. After several moments she says, "You're right. Nobody could expect you to understand." She thinks, and sighs. "It's hard to say it. A person . . . I—even though I was a drunk—I had to be myself in front of someone. Someone who meant the most to me. Someone I had to keep *with* me, all along the way. I can't expect you to understand—but it's the clearest sign there could ever be of how much I've loved you all this time. *You* were the one I loved, so *you* were the one who saw me drunk. It's horrible. It's what makes me feel the worst. But it's true, Sam. That's why."

He waits, then, in a very small voice, says, "I thought it was because the drinking was my fault. Because I caused it. I thought I had to be the one to see it because I made you do it by . . . by not being good enough."

She does not answer, except to squeeze him. He lets her hold him, and slowly he begins to shake.

Then the sobs come, and a wailing, reaching cry. She holds him. His back shudders as he cries, fighting each sob, until finally he lets go and the sobs rush from him.

She holds him as they stand, swaying slightly. His crying softens; the wails become whimpers, the quaking stops. In a while he is finished, and lets her hold him against her shoulder as he sniffs and sighs. It grows silent in the room. They stand as the sky outside the windows turns darker.

After a long time he straightens up, rubbing his eyes. He pulls back slightly, and looks around the room. He looks at her, but when he speaks it is as if he is talking only to himself: "Can *I* do that?"

"Do what, Sam?" she says softly.

He looks as if he has barely heard her. "Can I be myself in front of someone? In front of you?" His forehead is wrinkled, his eyes full of the question. "Can I just be your boy? Can I do it?"

Very gently, but firmly, she pulls his head back down against her chest. "You don't *do* it, Sam. You 'be' it. All you have to do is stop being what you think everybody *else* should be. Stop taking care of everything. And what you're left with is yourself."

After a moment, in a muffled voice he says, "I can't. I don't think I can stop."

"I said that too," she says. "I say it every day." She pulls his head up, and smiles into his face. "If we both stop, we'll be left with each other. Instead of just being alone." She wipes his cheek with a finger. "How does that sound?"

He looks at her for several moments. Then he lowers his head against her. She holds him long into the twilight.

E I G H T E E N

Sam jumps from the taxi the instant it has stopped, and hits the sidewalk at a run. As he cuts onto the front lawn the front door of the house is yanked open, and the Bigelows hurry out, buttoning coats.

The woman sees Sam and stops short, a look of fright on her face. Her husband looks up, sees Sam, and urges his wife toward the cab with his hand on her back. She continues to stare at Sam without greeting him, then looks down and hurries past.

The man points at Sam and says, "You wait here."

He walks the woman to the cab, helps her in, says something to the driver, and shuts the door. The cab waits. The man walks back to Sam.

"Mr. Bigelow," says Sam, extending his hand, "I want to offer my congratulations and explain why I left the papers instead of delivering them more ceremoniously. See, there was just so much to—"

"What happened to Ollie?" the man says plainly. He does not acknowledge Sam's hand.

Sam stammers. The man pinches the front of Sam's coat and tugs twice. "Wake up. No charming maturity now, please. This is serious: What happened to Ollie this afternoon?"

Sam, with a voice starting to shake, says, "I took him to see my mother."

The man nods. "I knew it." He lets go of Sam's coat. "You know what? Somebody should *spank* you. You think about why." He sighs. "Go on."

Sam frowns. "Just tell me if he's all right."

"No, he's not all right. He's in a lot of trouble, and in thirty seconds his parents will be on their way to get him out of it. Now, tell me a few things. First, how long have you been taking him to this church?"

"I never took him to any church. I know I insisted he be allowed out at night, but I had no idea—"

"Look," says the man, "I know that kids like you—alcoholics' kids—have a tough time telling the truth. But this is not the time for being creative. Tell me how long you've been taking him to church."

"Why does it have to be me?"

"Because he's ten years old and kids that age don't do this kind of thing by themselves. And *we* don't take him to those weirdo vigilante churches, do we? His brother made us promise we wouldn't 'affiliate' him in any way."

"Exactly," says Sam. "So why would *I* take him?"

"I couldn't possibly imagine," the man says, "but that doesn't mean you didn't do it. You're a deep creek, boy, and there's a lot going on underwater. I couldn't begin to figure out the currents, know what I mean? But forget it for the moment. Tell me something else: What happened with your mother?"

"She was drunk."

"Great," the man says. He sighs. "You poor kids. What else?"

"Ollie pulled out his saxophone and kind of played it at my mother. He . . . it was as if he expected her to do something when he played. When she didn't, he got upset and recited a bunch of the Steemer church doctrine about how alcohol is the stuff the devil uses to attract weak souls. Then he hit my mother with the saxophone." Sam hesitates; the man says nothing. "She's all right, though."

"Well, Ollie's not. He's downtown at a church,

locked in the bell tower, giving *sermons.* Hollering all this fancy language out into the street. The man who called us is the pastor or prior or whatever; he copied our number once off Ollie's saxophone case, though he never thought to use it. He says Ollie has attracted quite a crowd and has them really stoked up." The man shakes his head and laughs once. "The prior excused himself by saying Ollie isn't preaching *his* church's things; he's blowing off all this hot-blooded violent stuff he picked up somewhere else. He said Ollie's been coming to see him for a couple of months, but the kid 'never listened.' Says *he* would have helped Ollie. Which of course lets the guy off the hook."

Sam says, "You ask him if he's ever met me. Ask him if I ever brought Ollie."

"Maybe not," says the man. He studies Sam. "I told you yesterday I thought Ollie knew. Even so, I didn't expect him to *do* anything." He pauses. "I guess Ollie surprised both of us."

Sam nods. "I guess so."

"And you're not used to people surprising you. You usually have all the angles figured. This isn't the way things are *supposed* to happen."

"No," says Sam. "I'm not used to it."

The man nods. He puts a hand on Sam's shoulder. "You're a smart kid, Sam. But not that smart."

He turns and walks quickly toward the taxi. When he opens the door, he looks back at Sam.

"I don't know about all this alcohol business. You said that's one reason you picked us—we weren't part of the 'institutionalization.' So I'm not sure how much of this trouble has anything to do with your mother and her drinking. But Ollie's going to get help if he needs it. Next year his school is starting that AO program you wanted to steer him away from. He'll be in it."

"I really think he'd be better off if—"

"Thanks for your views, Sam, but they don't have the old dazzle right now, you know? I told you yesterday: This little showdown you arranged was the last fling for your judgment. It's our show now with Ollie. We are his *parents.*"

"Thanks to whose judgment?" says Sam with a quick, wry smile.

The man nods. "Yes. You're right. I have to be grateful for some of your judgment. As I just said, you're a smart kid. But nobody's smart enough to do *every*thing." He pauses. "Are you and your mother going to live together?"

"Yes," says Sam.

"Good luck," says the man. He gets in and closes the door. The taxi starts to pull away, then stops. The man's window rolls down.

"I don't want this to sound too harsh. I'm angry and I'm in a hurry, so I don't have time to sweeten it. So listen: We'd appreciate it if you gave us a few months with just our new family," the man says. "You know—a chance to sort things out, get used to the new commitments."

"I understand," says Sam. He thinks for a moment, frowning. He starts to speak a couple of times, but stops. Finally, he nods to himself, his face clears slightly, and he takes a deep breath. "I . . . I'm going to kind of have a new family of my own," he says.

"I guess you are."

Sam nods, still thinking. "I'll have stuff to sort out too. Commitments, all that stuff. Like you guys."

"Right," says the man, watching him carefully.

Sam sighs, frowns, nods. "I guess . . ." He hesitates.

"What, Sam? Say it."

"I guess," says Sam, "I guess maybe I won't have time." His eyes are suddenly full of tears. His voice is small and cracked; he speaks as if he cannot believe he is saying this: "I won't have time to take care of Ollie. I guess you'll have to do it."

The man says, "That's what parents are for, Sam."

Sam nods, blinking, clamping his mouth against a sob.

After a moment, the man says, "You come around

when you're all set to be just a brother again, okay?"

Sam nods.

The man doesn't roll up the window. "In the meantime—any message for Ollie?"

"Yes," says Sam clearly. The tears have receded. "Tell him I meant to, you know, tell him myself about all of this—about my mother, about . . ." He stops, and thinks. Then he says, "I don't know. Just . . . just tell him I tried." He waits. "Tried—to do too much."

The man watches him; then he waves, and says, "No kidding." The window goes up. The car rolls away.

FIC
BRO

C. 1

Brooks, Bruce.

No kidding.

$13.89   30401000500011

DATE			